GW00359981

K. SEAN HARRIS

DEATH
INCARNATE

Terri is determined to catch the serial rapist.
Even if she has to use herself as bait...

Cover Design by: Sanya Dockery
Book Design, Layout & Typesetting by: Sanya Dockery
Edited by: Sitara English

Published by: Book Fetish

www.kseanharris.com

Printed in the U.S.A.   ISBN: 978-976-610-808-3

My heart goes out to any woman that has ever been raped.

ALSO BY K. SEAN HARRIS:

Novels

Queen of the Damned

Kingdom of Death

Blood of Angels

Kiss of Death

The Garrison

The Heart Collector

The Stud

The Stud 11

Merchants of Death

Anthologies

The Sex Files

The Sex Files Vol. 2

Erotic Jamaican Tales

More Erotic Jamaican Tales

*For a testament is of force after men are dead:
otherwise it is of no strength at all while the
testator liveth.*

HEBREWS 9: 17

*And almost all things are by the law purged
with blood; and without shedding of blood is
no remission.*

HEBREWS 9: 22

Prologue

"Oh Tony! He's so beautiful," Terri breathed, tired but elated and emotional as she laid eyes on the life to which she had just given birth. Anthony beamed as he handed the crying baby boy to his fiancé.

"Si...he's the spitting image of his handsome padre," he said, grinning from ear to ear.

"Tony I'm so happy!" Terri cried, overwhelmed with joy. She couldn't wait for them to get married and start enjoying their life together as a family.

The scene then abruptly changed.

Terri was now holding a gun at Anthony in a hotel room. Her palms were sweaty and the beat of her heart was a loud thud to her ears.

"Put the gun down Tony...it's over...no more killing," Terri pleaded, knowing it would end badly. Anthony would never allow her to take him in.

"Do you really think you can kill me? Huh Terri?" Anthony asked softly as he advanced towards her.

Terri took an involuntary step back.

"Tony please...don't come any closer or I'm going to shoot...back-up is on the way. There is no way out. Please...just surrender."

Anthony kept smiling as he continued to approach her, his handsome face sporting a sad smile. "It was good, wasn't it T? But as they say, all good things must come to an end."

They both fired simultaneously.

Terri woke up screaming. Her baby-T and boy shorts were soaked with perspiration. Her throat felt parched. Her head was pounding painfully. Migraines. They always accompanied her dreams. Terri sighed in frustration as she wondered how much longer the dreams would continue. She had been having them at least once a week since the baby was born fifteen months ago. They frightened her with their vividness and intensity. She wondered if she should seek professional help. But which doctor could she trust? If it ever came out that she was seeing a psychiatrist it could seriously hurt her career and reputation; especially if the *reason* why she was seeing one was known. The baby's cries interrupted her thoughts. He always cried whenever she woke up screaming. She got up quickly to tend to him.

Chapter 1

"Oh god," the woman said in a hoarse whisper. "Please...I beg you...don't do this..."

The man to whom she was speaking smiled condescendingly as if she were a wayward child refusing to eat her vegetables though it was good for her. He ran his hands through her hair. It was limp and slick with sweat. He continued to smile in the face of her terror as he looked at her critically. Her smooth, oval face, though contorted with fear, was attractive. Large, soulful eyes; creamy caramel skin and a sexy mole just above the left side of her full lips made her very easy on the eyes. She was about five feet tall and very petite. Her height and weight, along with her innocent face, made her seem a lot younger than her thirty two years. He had gone through her pocketbook while she was still unconscious. A man could tell a lot about a woman by looking through her pocketbook. It is said that the eyes are windows to the soul, but when it comes to women, he begged to differ.

"God can't help you now sweetheart," he told her calmly as his eyes roamed over her slender but appealing body. His face wore a curious blend of lust and disgust. She was naked and her hands were tied to the bedpost.

Donna Parchment shivered and turned her head away from his indecipherable gaze. She could not comprehend why this was happening to her. One minute she was in the parking lot of the mall where she worked as an assistant manager at a pharmacy about to get into her car and head home, and the next thing she knew, she was about to become a statistic. She tried to recall what happened prior to her blacking out. The attractive, well-dressed man had approached her in the parking lot. "Excuse me, Miss," he had said pleasantly. "Do you know how to get to Tangerine Place?"

"Yes," she had replied, pausing with one foot into her car. "Just …"

He had moved so swiftly she hadn't gotten a chance to react. He had grabbed her and placed a handkerchief over her nose. She had struggled vainly for six seconds before losing consciousness. She had awakened to find herself in a brightly lit room, naked and tied to a bed, with her attacker sitting next to her. The room was small and windowless. The only piece of furniture was the wrought iron bed on which she was imprisoned. There was also a video camera on a tripod a few feet away from the bed. She had no idea how long she had been unconscious or where he had taken her. She started to cry as she wondered if she would ever see her son again. The thought brought on a panic attack and she started screaming and tugging on the ropes, which dug into her wrists painfully as she thrashed wildly on the bed. She kicked at her unwelcome host and her left foot struck him in the face.

He got up off the bed and looked at her. He was smiling but his eyes held no warmth. They were as cold as a December night on the Blue Mountain peak. He casually rubbed his jaw.

"You can scream all you want. This is a sound proof room. All you will accomplish is pain…unlike anything you've ever felt before."

His words made her scream even more. She screamed even louder when his large fist smashed into her right eye.

Chapter 2

erri was at home watching Marc-Anthony, her fifteen month old son, sleeping peacefully in his crib when her cell phone rang. She checked the caller ID. It was the Commissioner of Police.

"Hello, Sir," Terri said, wondering what had happened for the Commissioner to be calling her this late. It was 11:55 p.m.

"There has been another rape," he said without preamble, "even more brutal than the previous two. This time, the victim was murdered."

Terri was silent. Three rapes in ten days in Kingston. One every three days. Each more brutal than the last. Terri sighed as she looked at her son. Ever since she had removed herself from frontline duty and taken up an administrative post since the birth of her son, the Commissioner, the general public, and several newspaper columnists, have been clamouring for her to reconsider. She was simply the best cop in the island. Perhaps the western hemisphere, some would argue. She had taken a desk job because God forbid if something should happen to her, her child would be an orphan. It was bad enough he would grow up without ever knowing his dad, but to lose his mother would be nothing short of tragic.

"We need to catch this bastard, Terri," the Commissioner continued earnestly. "He's smart and he doesn't seem like he plans to slow down anytime soon. I need you to reconsider. This case requires your analytical skills and your tenacity. You have to get back out in the field and catch this sadistic maniac."

"I'll meet with you and the current lead detective on the case at 9 a.m. in the morning," Terri told him resignedly.

"Thanks, Terri, I knew you would do the right thing," the Commissioner said, relieved that she had agreed. If anyone could catch this rapist, it would be Terri Miller. She was the smartest and most persistent person he had ever met. Her quick, meteoric rise through the ranks was unprecedented. He was sure she would eventually become Jamaica's first female Commissioner of Police. Terri was like a daughter to him. He had taken an active interest in her career from the moment she had entered the force a little over five years ago.

Terri smiled ruefully. Her mentor knew her as well as her parents did, maybe even more. He knew which buttons to push. They had gotten quite close upon her return to the island after taking an extended vacation to give birth to Marc-Anthony at a private clinic in Florida. Her best friend, Anna, had accompanied her. Her parents had wanted to make the trip as well but things had been strained between them and Terri due to their initial negative response to her pregnancy. Her mother had almost had a stroke that her well-bred, upper-class daughter would have a child out of wedlock, and to add insult to injury, would divulge no information about the mystery father. They now loved their only grandchild to death.

"See you tomorrow," Terri told him and terminated the call. She went over to the large window and looked out at the lovely view. Kingston, at night, was a very breathtaking sight. Terri thought about how her life would change once she resumed frontline duty. She had gotten used to coming home early and spending loads of time with her precious bundle of joy. He was the spitting image of his father. Terri still had mixed emotions whenever she thought of her child's father, Anthony Garcia. She still loved him and still cried occasionally whenever she thought of the way things had turned out. The shootout between them at the hotel a little over a year ago still played in her head like a horror flick every now and then. Usually at night. In her dreams. Killing the man she loved and the father of her child had been a very traumatic experience. Adding to the despair and the trauma was the fact that he had turned out to be a cold-blooded murderer and a drug trafficker.

She walked over to the crib and picked up Marc-Anthony. He was a sinfully pretty baby. He had his father's jet-black curly hair and unusual grey eyes, and had inherited his mother's thin, aristocratic features. He would be devastatingly handsome when he got older. Just like his dad, the handsome but deadly half-Latino who had captured her heart.

The baby's cries awakened Maria out of her deep slumber. She stirred and looked over at her husband. He was dead to the world. He would remain like that until she woke him up at 5 a.m. His shift at Kingston's, and perhaps Jamaica's finest hospital, Caribbean University Hospital, began at 6. She planned to let him work there for another year and a half before pressuring him to start a private practice. He would then be 45 years old and those long dreadful hours he was currently working would take too much of a toll on him. A private practice would be much more lucrative and he would set his own hours, leaving him more time to rest and to spend with his family. She got up and padded to the baby's room.

"Is my little *querido hijo* hungry…hmmm?" Maria cooed as she lifted Diego from his crib. He cried harder in response. Muttering sweet nothings to him, she went into the kitchen to feed her prince. Diego, apparently seeing that his mother was about to do something about his hunger, ceased crying and watched silently as she placed some apple-flavoured Gerber baby food in his SpongeBob bowl. Maria thought about her life as she sat on a stool next to the kitchen counter and fed Diego. She considered herself to be the luckiest woman in the world. It was nothing short of amazing the way things had turned out. After being raped and sodomized by Hernanadez's goons and near death, Anthony had come to her rescue and taken her to the hospital, saving her life. Then, as fate would have it, the doctor who attended to her fell madly in love with her. Not even after she told him about her former lifestyle and horrible experiences, albeit a slightly watered down version, had he wavered in his affection. The big test had been telling him that she was pregnant. She had been certain that would have been too much for the poor man to swallow. Thankfully, she had been wrong.

He had taken her in, used his contacts within the government to secure her papers which allowed her to remain in the country legally, and had proposed to her. Grateful and thankful, she had accepted without hesitation. She would never be able to love him the way he obviously loved her, a love so strong that he would overlook all the baggage she came with, emotional and other-wise, and want her to be his wife, but she was sure that she would be a loyal and a dutiful wife to him. They had gotten married at his best friend's villa in lush, beautiful Portland in a small, intimate ceremony. She thought of Anthony as she looked at her son, his unusual grey eyes merry now that he was being fed. He looked just like his father. She was thankful Anthony had left a piece of himself behind. *Que su alma descance en paz.* May his soul rest in peace.

Chapter 3

erri got to police headquarters at 8 a.m. She was dressed in a fitted, black, pinstripe pants suit and trendy Juicy Couture black pumps. Mavis, her longtime helper, had been receptive to Terri's request that she started living with her as she would now need someone there at all times to take care of Marc-Anthony. Going back on frontline duty meant working long hours and having to leave home on a moment's notice. Mavis' twenty year old daughter would pack some of her things and bring to her at Terri's house during the course of the day. With that settled, Terri could now focus on getting herself acquainted with all the evidence gathered from the three crime scenes. First up would be the 9 a.m. meeting with the lead detectives on the case, and the Commissioner.

"Good morning, Asst. Superintendent," Mrs. Green, Terri's secretary said when Terri entered the reception area. "I heard you are back on frontline duty, that's great."

"Good morning, Mrs. Green," Terri responded pleasantly, adding as she ignored Mrs. Green's last remark, "I need a strong cup of coffee."

Terri chuckled and shook her head as she sat behind her expansive desk. The office grapevine was something else. They probably knew she was back on frontline duty even before she had made the decision. The Commissioner had left a thin file on her desk. She started reading the material immediately and didn't look up when the secretary knocked on the door and brought in the coffee. The man was a monster. A sick, clever monster. Though the first two victims had survived, they had both been drugged with chloroform and diethyl ether, and remembered nothing about the details of their attack. The first victim had woken up at a deserted bus stop in the volatile Maxfield area in the wee hours of the morning. A good Samaritan from the community, a taxi driver, about to turn in for the night, had given her a ride home. She hadn't gone to the police until three days later, after hearing on the news what happened to another woman and by then, the only evidence that was left was the residue of the drugs in her system. The second victim had woken up groggy and in pain on the ground in the parking lot of a mall on Red Hills road, eight hours after she had left work, and had flagged down a passing patrol car which had taken her to the hospital where it was confirmed that she had been brutally raped.

The third victim. Terri's heart went out to her and her family. She must have suffered unimaginable horrors at the hands of the rapist before he took her life. The report stated that the woman's body, discovered by two fourth graders taking a shortcut to school through an open lot in the Liguanea area, had been terribly mutilated. Terri gasped as she looked at the pictures. The woman's right eye had been gouged out, her nose had been smashed flat, her neck and ribs had been broken, and there was appalling evidence which suggested that the rapist had had sex with her before and after her death. Terri sighed and closed the file. This was not good. She had never before seen so many different characteristics in the actions of one rapist. She would have to create a new profile for the guy. She swiveled her large, comfortable leather chair to face the window and looked out at the bustling metropolis of New Kingston, the business hub of the Caribbean. Police Headquarters, formerly located at Old Hope Road was now on Holborn Road, housed in Jamaica Towers, the largest and tallest building in the entire island. Terri's office, along with the Commissioner of Police and the Assistant Commissioner of Police, was on the twelfth floor. The rapist was down there somewhere, waiting to strike again. Presumably in two days.

I'm coming to get you, Terri mused as she sipped her coffee. *Don't know how yet, but I'm going to get you...count on that.* She checked the time and gathered her things. It was three minutes to nine. The meeting was being held in the conference room on the eleventh floor. Terri and the Commissioner exited their offices at the same time and exchanged pleasantries as they took the elevator down to the eleventh floor. Everyone was there waiting when they arrived.

"Good morning," the Commissioner said in his deep, gravelly baritone. "Let's get right down to business. Assistant Superintendent Miller is back on the frontline and will assume responsibility for the case with immediate effect."

Detective Corporal Ronald Stern, the lead detective on the case up until the Commissioner's remarks, did not hide his displeasure. This was the biggest case of his career and now the Commissioner was letting this bitch steal his thunder. Terri noticed the nasty looks he was casting her way. She was stoic as she held eye contact until he averted his eyes. She was used to the male chauvinistic pigs that permeated the force at every level. They didn't faze her. Especially idiots like Ronald Stern. He was a fifteen year veteran of the force. And one could say, having attained the rank of Corporal, he had been promoted to the highest level of his incompetence. Terri considered him a common thug who thought that brawn instead of brains would get the job done. He had bungled more cases than she could care to remember. Suffice to say, he was way out of his depth on this one. Thankfully, the ever dependable Detective Foster had been a part of the team, hence the clear and concise report that the Commissioner had received and passed on to her. At least she had somewhere to start.

Ignoring Stern's hostile body language, the Commissioner continued, "I expect everyone to give her their full cooperation."

He then sat after gesturing for Terri to take the floor.

Terri stood and faced the large conference table that was now seating seven.

"First off, I'd like to commend the team for the good job done thus far. Gentlemen, time is of the essence. Jamaica is currently ranked number six in the world in rapes per capita…by the time this guy is through we'll be number one," Terri quipped. Everybody except Detective Corporal Stern gave a wry chuckle. "Based on my preliminary assessment of the rapist, he seems to be a rare specimen. He embodies some of the characteristics of three of the four rapist profiles: the power-assertive rapist, the anger-retaliation rapist and the anger-excitation rapist. These profiles are defined by motive, style of attack and psychosexual characteristics."

Terri paused and looked around the table at each of the men before continuing. They were paying rapt attention, even Stern, who was still scowling. Terri plowed ahead, ignoring the vibration of the blackberry pearl on her waist. "I think the perpetrator is athletic and has a "macho" image of himself. He also seems to feel animosity towards women and wants to punish and degrade them. He is also obviously a sadist who derives sexual gratification from inflicting pain. He is most likely charming and very intelligent. He is criminally sophisticated and will be extremely difficult to catch."

Terri then sat down and drank some of the water that had been placed on the table for the meeting.

"No one will comment about this case to the media. Any queries must be directed to me. I will be cutting down the core investigative team to just two members, myself and Detective Foster, any questions?"

You fucking bitch! Detective Corporal Stern thought angrily as he looked at Terri. He had hated the uppity, pedantic cunt from the moment she had become a member of the Police Force. He hoped the rapist got a hold of her. Now wouldn't that be something. The thought immediately made him feel better. The other detectives were merely disappointed that they wouldn't get to work closely with her. She was so smart and glamourous and beautiful. A rose in a garden of thorns.

"Well, that will be it then gentlemen," Terri said, after a pregnant pause. She gathered her things and rose. "Detective Foster, kindly report to my office for a follow up session."

Detective Foster nodded and Terri shook the Commissioner's hand and left the room, leaving behind a faint whiff of Angel by Thierry Mugler. The Commissioner was pleased as he checked the time. Now that Terri was at the helm, he was confident that sooner or later, there would be a breakthrough on the case. There was to be a press conference at 12 noon. Terri was scheduled to address the media for ten minutes.

"Have a seat," Terri said pleasantly when she and Detective Foster got to her office. They had not spoken and had only glimpsed each other at a distance since that fateful day, fifteen months ago, when she had the shoot-out with Anthony at the Regent Court hotel. He had been part of the back-up team that had come to her aid. "How have you been?"

"I'm good," Detective Foster replied. It was bitter sweet for him to be in her presence. He relished any opportunity to be near her but it also hurt his heart because he knew he could never be with her. She was way out of his league. There were so many things he wanted to say to her. He had always wondered about Terri's relationship with the man she had killed. He had never forgotten the anguish in her eyes, despite her bullet wound, as she held the dying man's hands, when he and the back-up team had burst into the hotel room. He heard she had a baby. Apparently no one knew who the father was and very few people had actually seen the child. "It's good to see you."

Terri smiled. "Thanks."

She knew the quiet, soft-spoken detective had a thing for her. Most men did, but she detected more than mere lust in his eyes. If he wasn't such a good detective and someone she felt she could trust, she would have never assigned him to work on the case with her but she knew she could count on him to maintain his professionalism.

"I think he will stick to his pattern…at least for now. That means he's going to strike again on Saturday evening," Terri said, switching gears, "in a parking lot."

Foster nodded gravely.

"We don't have the manpower to stake out all the parking lots in Kingston so I'm going to select four for us to monitor between the hours of five to seven. I'm going pull three patrol cars and eight officers to cover the designated parking lots. Thus far he has used the lots of two malls so we are going to focus on three in the Half-Way-Tree area and one in New Kingston. I don't think he's going to go to any of the two malls he went to previously." Terri twiddled her solid gold Parker pen between her manicured fingers. It wouldn't be nearly enough but she could only hope they would catch a break.

The man chuckled as he ate his lunch and watched the news conference, currently being broadcasted on the two local TV stations. Terri Miller was on, telling the nation not to worry, but that the women in Kingston should be careful until they caught this dangerous psychotic criminal who had decided to make their lives a living hell. He bristled at her description. Psychotic? He was as sane as she was. He just lived his life on a different level from everyone else. He lived on the edge and gave in to his cravings. He did not live in fear or restriction. The world was his playground and by God he would play. He considered himself a hero for the common man, so emasculated and marginalized by society that he felt inferior to women. He was here to tip back the balance of scale in favour of man. Show these bitches just who was in charge. *Don't you worry Supercop,* he mused as he chewed slowly, savouring every morsel of the spicy curry goat and white rice with boiled green bananas that he had prepared. *Your day will come.*

Chapter 4

He enjoyed cooking for himself and preparing three square meals a day. It was one of the things he had missed dearly when he was fighting for Uncle Sam in hot spots such as Iraq. Good Jamaican food. He always knew he would have returned to his homeland after his last tour ended. The army paid well, and after his decent base salary, he also received hardship pay and hostile fire pay. He had saved so much money while being stationed overseas that he was very well off after opting not to renew his contract. He had taken advantage of the Army's saving deposit program where they paid ten percent interest per annum. His net worth was close to half a million US dollars. Twelve years of fighting for Uncle Sam. He thought he came out pretty good. Certainly better than most. All those years of living below his means and saving his money, and the strength of the US dollar, would enable him to live like a king when he returned to Jamaica. He would be able to buy anything he wanted. The Major in charge of his unit had been disappointed that he wouldn't renew his contract with the army. After all, he was only 30 years old and had a bright future in the army ahead of him, having won a Silver Star and a Bronze Star Medal for bravery during his tenure. He had thoroughly enjoyed his time in the army, especially serving in Iraq. While many of his counterparts were afraid to be deployed to Iraq, he had welcomed it. To be able to rape and kill with near impunity? Priceless. He had raped and killed at least ten Iraqi women. Sent them screaming to Allah with their bodies bloody and violated. Under the guise of war, it was very easy to get away with certain atrocities. One day, he had been caught by a Sergeant Major as he raped a woman in the remnants of a bombed out house on the outskirts of Baghdad. After a moment's hesitation, with the woman pausing with his phallus deep in her mouth while the cold steel of his AK-47 was resting on her forehead, his superior had commented why should he have all of the fun and had joined in. That incident had brought home the fact that he was not alone. Others were just afraid. They needed someone to show them the way. He was that beacon of light in their darkness.

He hummed a tune by Lenny Kravitz as he placed the dishes in the dishwasher. Upon leaving the army, he immediately made plans to return to the island of his birth. He had scouted the internet for available housing in Kingston and had purchased a lovely two bedroom apartment in a gated complex in Liguanea Plains. He had also checked the feasibility of opening the security gadgets business he planned to operate and was pleased to discover that there was definitely a market for it. Crime was a big problem on the island and he was positive people would pay for the high-tech gadgets to make their lives safer. After six months of planning and setting things in place, he returned to Jamaica. It was a fresh start for him. He had migrated when he was four years old and had never been back. He had no friends here and he had not been in touch with any of his family members. A loner by nature, that was fine by him.

After arriving and settling into his apartment, he had spent a week relaxing at an adult all-inclusive resort in Negril. When he returned to Kingston, he purchased a Range Rover and spent the next three weeks driving around Kingston and its environs, acclimatizing himself to the city. Within a year, he had started his small but immensely profitable business, POW Electronic Security Company Ltd. He had a staff of eight and never went into office. He was plugged into the office electronically and was able to keep tabs on everything from the spare bedroom at home that he had converted into an office. The only employee who really knew him was the forty year old ex-policeman he had hired to be his general manager. The general manager was the first employee hired and he was the one charged to hire the rest of the staff. With money at his disposal and time on his hands, he had been ready to resume his mission. The first three women he had raped were just appetizers. He was just warming up.

He went into the bathroom to take a shower. He undressed and looked at his naked physique in the wall to wall mirror. *Pure muscle*, he thought admirably, *nothing but power*. Women always found him attractive and he could get his fair share easy enough but where was the fun in that? Where would be the power and utter domination? His mother had failed him miserably, effectively giving birth to his hatred for the so-called fairer sex. He could never have a meaningful relationship with a woman. They weren't worthy. There was only one way to deal with them. To make them understand that man was king. He had a large tattoo of a red-eyed grey wolf with blood dripping from its fangs spanning the right side of his chest down to his stomach. He caressed the vivid, ferocious-looking tattoo lovingly. The itch was still there and growing. He obtained a turgid erection just by thinking about his next victim. It was almost time to scratch the itch. In another two days.

Anna purred softly as she arched her back. She was in the offices of Rupert Walters Photography Inc., sitting on Rupert's large desk, with her long legs on Rupert's broad shoulders. His near-bald head was buried in her plump vagina, prickly with new growth as she hadn't shaved in three days. Her trendy Chloe summer dress was bunched around her tiny waist. She had come by to look at the pictures from the photo shoot that she had done with Rupert for the fashion spread of a new Caribbean lifestyle magazine. The pictures were fabulous and after two glasses of white wine to celebrate, Rupert had asked if he could taste her sweet Jamaican pussy. He was an Italian who had a love for the tropics and a reputation for being a photographer who tended to get the best out of his models. He had set up shop in Jamaica for two years now and though Anna had worked with him on several occasions, this was the first time he had attempted to mix business with pleasure. And pleasure it was indeed. Rupert had a thick, nimble tongue that knew how to extract pleasure from every crevice of her pussy. She had already climaxed twice.

Rupert got up and looked at her questioningly. Anna nodded. She thought it cute that he would ask permission to penetrate her. Technically he was right though; he had only asked to *taste* her. Rupert then took out his dick and quickly rolled on a condom. It reminded Anna of one of those thick German sausages that she had tried when she was in Stuttgart for a fashion show last year. She slid off the desk and turned around. As Rupert readied himself and entered her, she glanced at the clock on the wall and realized that it was 1 p.m. She had missed Terri's press conference. She had tried calling Terri earlier but her phone had just rang out. She wanted to know if the rumors were true that Terri was back in the field. She was peeved that she wasn't the first to hear. After all, she was Terri's best friend. She moaned loudly and spread her legs wider as Rupert settled into a nice rhythm. His dick felt almost as good as his tongue. Almost.

Chapter 5

"Bwoy mi ah tell yuh, life nuh fair ah bloodclaat," Detective Corporal Ronald Stern bemoaned to his two closest friends on the Force as they took their seats in the large cafeteria on the ground floor. The cafeteria was run by a restaurant that had been given the contract when Police Headquarters was relocated to its posh, new digs. The food was excellent, though the top brass never ate there. "Dat fucking bitch just come tek over de case, just like dat."

Detective Foster, who was sitting at the table next to Stern with a female constable that liked him, cringed at Stern's words. How dare he talk about Terri like that? The man was a reprobate. Unfit to carry a badge. Foster tried to ignore him and concentrate on what the woman was saying. She was telling him about a new movie opening over the weekend that she wanted to see.

"Ah so it go still enuh," the one everyone called Eastwood, after the famous gunslinger in the Western movies of old, commiserated. He was a revered marksman and even the most hardened gunman was wary of him. No one wanted to be in a shootout with Eastwood. "Pussy is power."

Detective Corporal Stern laughed brashly. "Damn bitch not even know ah who ah de father of her pickney. Uptown whore."

He and his comrades cackled at that.

Detective Foster had heard enough. Just as his lunch companion, seeing that Foster was not taking a hint, was about to ask him if he would take her to the movies when he turned in his chair and addressed Stern coldly.

"Shut the fuck up Stern and have some respect, she is your superior," Foster told him in a steely tone.

"Pussyhole!" Stern thundered rising from his chair as the rest of the cafeteria went silent. "I am *your* fucking superior. So who yuh t'ink yuh talking to like that?"

Detective Foster rose from his chair as well and they stood inches apart.

Stern's breath was rancid as he continued to rant in Foster's face. "Yuh want mi fi box dung yuh bloodclaat?"

Foster did not respond. He was just waiting for Stern to lay a finger on him. Stern outweighed him by a good thirty pounds but Foster knew he could whip his ass in a fair fight. Though he wanted to, he hoped it wouldn't come to that. The scene was embarrassing enough as it is. The cafeteria was packed and they were the center of attention.

"Ah mussi pussy yuh a look," Stern said as Eastwood pulled him away from Foster. "She nuh want yuh...so nuh waste yuh time punk."

His words stung Foster more than he would ever know. Foster took a deep breath and turned away from Stern and his chuckling friends as he tried to control himself. He wanted to punch Stern in his smelly mouth so bad he could cry. Instead, he touched his stunned lunch companion on her shoulder as a goodbye gesture and left his unfinished lunch and the taunting words of Stern behind. He knew the talk amongst the rank and file officers would be how Stern had disrespected and embarrassed him and he didn't do anything about it. Well, as far as he was concerned he had stood up to Stern which is more than he could say for several others who Stern had bullied one way or another over the years. He knew he had to watch his back from now on though. Stern was the type of person to carry a grudge and he was an idiot. That, in Foster's book, made him a dangerous man.

Terri was at Rob's Steakhouse having barbecued spareribs for lunch when an attractive, well-dressed woman came up to her table. Terri was lunching alone.

"Hi Terri!" the woman gushed. "It's so nice to see you."

Terri smiled quizzically at the woman and her companion, a muscular clean-cut younger guy. "Hi, how are you?" she responded, trying to figure out who the woman was.

"You don't remember me do you?" the woman asked smiling. "It's ok, don't be embarrassed. I would have been surprised if you had recognized me immediately. I'm Elaine Johnson, you knew me then as Elaine Mayweather."

Terri's eyes bulged in shock. Elaine Mayweather. She had killed her brute of a husband in self-defense during a domestic dispute at their home fifteen months ago. Her husband, who had been the Assistant Commissioner of Police at the time of his demise, had also been deeply involved with criminal elements. The Jamaica Police Force had endured many corruption scandals in its time, but because of Mayweather's high-level status, that one had rocked the nation. The transformation was remarkable. The woman Terri remembered had been withdrawn, overweight and had no sense of style. The woman before her was a complete contrast.

"Wow," Terri said, "you look absolutely fabulous."

"Thank you," Elaine responded, smiling broadly. "This is my husband, Howard Johnson."

Terri shook the young man's hand. *Good for you Elaine*, Terri mused. Apparently things had turned out very well for her after her husband's death.

Terri invited them to join her and for the next forty minutes, Elaine entertained her with colourful stories about her various cosmetic surgeries, her wedding – they had gotten married in Paris – and her trips to Europe, Cancun and Bali. Terri remembered that vast sums of money had been discovered in several accounts upon Mayweather's death – no doubt the proceeds from his illegal activities. Terri had frozen some of the accounts but had left a substantial amount for the widow to access. After all she had been through she deserved it.

After his shower, the man moisturized his entire physique and padded in the nude to his office, which he referred to as the control room, where he sat at his huge desk and looked at the large television screen in front of him. He could monitor everything at his business place. The receptionist, a young nubile beauty that he knew was fucking her much older general manager, was sitting on the toilet seat. She was talking on her cell phone. He turned on the audio. Based on her side of the conversation, she was gossiping with one her girlfriends about Patrick Gordon, the general manager. Apparently Gordon had promised to help her get a car for her birthday which was coming up in two weeks. She told her girlfriend that if Patrick reneged on his promise, she was going to tell his wife about their affair. *Manipulating little whore*, he thought disgustedly. He sighed as he remembered the day he had discovered that his mother was a prostitute.

Chapter 6

He was nine years old at the time and had come home early from school on that life-changing Monday afternoon. If his mother hadn't been busy servicing clients from 8 a.m. that morning, she would have seen on the news that there had been a shooting just a few meters from her son's school and that they had decided to send the kids home early. Instead, she had serviced six clients, and was in the process of earning $250 with two potbellied Caucasian men, when her son, hearing inhumane sounds emanating from his mother's bedroom, had opened the door. He would never forget the sight on his mother's rumpled bed.

No one saw him at first, as their backs were to the entrance of the bedroom. His mother had been astride one man, facing him, while the other was behind her, deeply embedded in her anus. Though she was grunting and screaming loudly, she seemed to be enjoying herself. He wasn't sure how long he had stood there gaping, frozen with shock, as his young impressionable mind struggled to comprehend the scene before him, when the man behind his mother got up so that they could change positions and turned and saw him.

"Who the fuck is this rug rat?" the man had commented, looking at him with a bemused expression.

His mother had turned around and walked over to him angrily, unconcerned about her nakedness. She slapped him viciously.

"Don't you know that you must knock before entering a closed room? Huh?" She slapped him again for good measure. "And what the hell are you doing home so early?"

"Hey bitch, we didn't pay to watch you discipline your son, get your ass back over here," the man who had spoken earlier demanded.

"I'll deal with you later," his mother snarled, jabbing a finger to his forehead and went back over to the two men.

Young Carlton Watson remained rooted to the spot and watched as the man who had spoken roughly penetrated his mother from behind, gripping a fistful of her hair painfully. She groaned and opened wide as the other man placed his large member in her mouth. Maybe another child would have run away from the depraved scene. But not him. It had stirred something in him. Aside from realizing that he now hated his mother with a passion, he also was very excited at the rough manner in which the men were treating her. He watched until it was over.

Chapter 7

eing back on frontline duty, and especially due to the nature of the case she was currently investigating, made Terri wonder if her home was secure enough. Suppose someone, trying to get to her, kidnapped or harmed her son? It was a gated complex with two armed guards but one could never be too careful. So after lunch, she had borrowed a phone book from one of the waiters at the restaurant and browsed through the section where the security firms were located. She decided to check out two that were in the Half-Way-Tree area. She checked the time. It was 2:10 p.m. She had a little over an hour to spare before her 3:30 appointment. She was due at the Constant Spring police station to supervise a very important ID parade. The cop in charge of the station had requested her presence as he thought that her being there would sooth the fears of the witness. If the witness failed to identify the suspect, the murderer of a family of three which took place two weeks ago in the war-torn community of August Town, would walk free.

Watson was doing some online banking when he casually glanced at the screen showing the office. He gave it his undivided attention and turned on the audio when he realized that none other than Terri Miller was speaking with one of the sales representatives. What the hell was she doing at his business place?

"Hi Ms. Miller," Roger the sales representative attending to Terri said pleasantly. It was his first time seeing the popular police-woman in person and she was even more beautiful up close. "How can I be of assistance?"

"Hello," Terri replied. "I'm interested in seeing your latest line of home security gadgets."

Watson listened from his home sixty-five miles away attentively. He knew that it could not have been anything associated with her investigation. There was no way she could connect him to any of the rapes and the murder. He listened on.

"You've definitely come to the right place, Ms. Miller," Roger informed her as he led her to the small conference room where they dealt with important clients. "I'm sure we have something for your needs."

Terri followed him into the room and for the next ten minutes, she browsed with him through the company's catalogue. They did have some impressive, high-tech gadgets. Terri selected a wireless alarm system that once triggered at home, would beep in her automobile and at her office if she so desired. It also came with a video monitoring system that would place cameras anywhere she wished in the apartment, linked to a handheld wi-fi set that she could take anywhere with her. It was perfect. And very expensive. It would cost one hundred and fifty thousand dollars, inclusive of installation. Terri used her platinum visa credit card to pay for it and Roger happily informed her that it could be installed the very next day. Terri promised to fax them instructions as to where she would want the cameras placed, as well as her address. She told Roger that someone would be there so they could go as soon as they received the set-up instructions. Upbeat about her purchase, Terri then made her way quickly to her SUV. Traffic was a bitch heading up to Constant Spring and she didn't want to be late for the ID parade.

Watson watched as she sashayed out to the parking lot. Even he had to admit that Terri Miller was an incredible-looking woman. He couldn't detect a physical flaw - other than the fact that she was a woman. He chuckled at that. Terri Miller had just provided him with the opportunity to enter her home. He could feel his adrenaline flowing. What luck! Goes to show the gods were on his side. He would inform the general manager that he would personally take care of the Terri Miller job. God he couldn't wait. Terri was going to get a bit more than she paid for. He was going to put hidden cameras all over the apartment. As of tomorrow, as long as she was home, he would be able to watch her every move. The thought made him giddy with excitement. He flipped open a cabinet filled with DVDs and took out the one labeled 'Brooklyn-March 05'. It was one of his favourites. He had taped his brutal rape of a young co-ed who attended City College in Brooklyn. He had rented a room at a small hotel for three days and had hooked up a camera to record any attacks he managed to carry out. The girl, whom he had met at a bar, had gone to the hotel with him willingly enough, but had changed her mind once she got to the room and he told her he only wanted oral and anal. He had showed her in no uncertain terms that no was not an option. He had no idea if she ever reported the incident as he was on a plane to start his new life in Jamaica bright and early the next morning, leaving the girl unconscious in the room.

He thought of Terri Miller as he lubed his turgid member with massage oil. He masturbated as he watched himself in brutal action from two years ago. His excitement mounted and he turned up the volume, filling the room with the woman's screams. He climaxed the same time he climaxed onscreen.

Chapter 8

erri got home at 8 p.m. later that day. She was very anxious to see Marc-Anthony. It was the first time she had ever been away from him for so long. She knew he was in good hands with Mavis, but she had missed him terribly. He was sleeping when she got home but as if sensing his mother's presence in the room, he woke up and she played with him until he fell asleep again. She then walked around the house, deciding where to put the cameras. She decided to put one on the patio and the other in the baby's room. She didn't think anymore was needed in the house. There was no need to have Mavis under surveillance. She went into the small den next to her bedroom and faxed all the necessary information to POW Electronics. They would see it when they got in first thing in the morning. She then told Mavis to expect an electronic technician to come by tomorrow to do an installation.

She then took a long, luxurious bath while she listened to the new Alicia Keyes album, after which she had some lasagna and white wine for supper. She returned Anna's call when she was through.

"Hello sweetie," Anna said, as she looked over herself in the mirror. She was going to an album release party for one of Jamaica's newest singing sensations. She had gotten invited by the singer's publicist, as she was known to be part of Kingston's "in-crowd". She was wearing a skin-tight Dior jumper which she knew was going to grab all the attention. Jumpers were going to make a big comeback and she was positive she was the only one in Jamaica who owned any of the new designs as they were just about to be released in Europe. She was an A-list model, so she regularly received gifts from some of the top designers world-wide. "I'm here getting ready to attend an album release party. I had called you earlier but I guess you were busy…seeing as you're back in the field and all."

Terri chuckled inwardly. She knew that tone. Anna was peeved that she hadn't been the first to know about her decision.

"It happened very suddenly honey," Terri said soothingly. "I decided during a late night conversation with the Commissioner last night and then I was really busy today."

"Ok…so how does it feel? Are you ok?" Anna asked, as she grabbed her matching Dior pocketbook and turned off the bed-room light.

"I'm fine. I missed Marc-Anthony a lot today though," Terri replied.

"Awww….how is my handsome god-son?" she asked, pausing by the base for the cordless phone.

"He's great."

"Ok, hun, I've got to go…the launch started an hour ago so it's time for me to make my grand entrance," Anna said airily.

Terri laughed. Anna was something else. "Ok, I'll catch up with you soon."

"Love you…bye." Anna placed the phone on the base to charge and left the apartment.

After speaking with Anna, Terri flipped through the channels and settled on CBS. CSI Miami, her favourite TV show, was up next.

Carlton Watson was on his second drink, listening to the eclectic sounds of Reality X, Jamaica's newest reggae singing sensation, when Anna walked in, creating quite a stir. He had been invited to the launch, by a client of his, who happened to own the record label to which Reality X was signed. The client had purchased security equipment for both his home and his recording studio. The invitation had invited "The Manager" of POW Electronics but when Patrick Gordon, the general manager, had sent up some things from the office for him, and he had listened to the marketing CD containing four songs that was packaged with the invitation, he had decided to attend. He loved the rock-fused reggae beats that the singer favoured. Real cutting-edge stuff. He could appreciate that. And so did North America and England, where Reality X's lead single had shot to the top of the pop charts. It was only then, did he get the recognition he deserved in Jamaica, where most people had dismissed his sound as "rock" and "alternative music".

Anna glided around the room and hugged and shook hands of those she knew. The formalities were now over and everyone was just relaxing and having a good time. Watson watched her intently from the right corner of the bar. She was tall and exotic-looking, a very attractive woman. He figured if she wasn't a model she should have been one. He liked her trendy jumper. He would love to slice it off of her slender body as she shivered with fear. She loved being the center of attention. He could see that. He hated that. Probably thought she was better than people. He noted the way she barely said hi to certain people. He felt the beginning of an erection as he thought of all the things he would like to do to her. Cut her smug, it's-all-about-me-ass right down to size. She was lucky that he was in control at the moment. Or tonight would've been a night for her to remember. If he allowed her to live. He smiled as he sipped his Jack Daniels on the rocks. He had just spared her life and she didn't know even know it. Maybe the next time he saw her she wouldn't be so lucky.

Chapter 9

Maria got up early on Friday morning. She had several errands to run on the road and she wanted to be done by early afternoon. After preparing her husband's breakfast and sending him off to work, she gave Rita, the helper, some instructions and then got herself and Diego ready to hit the road. By eight-thirty she was on her way to her dental appointment which was at nine.

Watson, having seen Terri's fax when he got home in the wee hours of the morning– everything that got faxed to his office also came through at his house – called the number provided at 8:30, after he had showered and had breakfast. The helper answered the phone. He told her he would be there to do the installation at nine-thirty. That was fine with Mavis as she had planned to go to the supermarket around midday. Surely the technician would be done by then.

Anna woke up feeling extremely fatigued and dehydrated.
Someone had introduced her to Reality X at the launch and she
went club hopping with him and his entourage after the launch.
Reality X and his crew were into designer drugs and Anna
popped ecstasy pills with them as they danced up a storm at three
clubs before going to a mansion in Jacks Hill where Reality X
was staying. They had practically fucked all night, fueled by the
energy of the dangerous drug. Now she was feeling like shit.
Groaning, she crawled out of bed and staggered to the bathroom
where she took a very cold shower. It helped somewhat and she
threw on one of Reality X's t-shirts and went into the kitchen to
make a concoction that a bartender friend of hers had taught her
many years ago. She hoped all the ingredients were there. It
would definitely pick her up.

Having informed Gordon that he would be handling the
installation at Terri Miller's home personally, Watson headed out
to the complex where Terri's house was located. He was in a very
good mood. Every man in Jamaica, even the homosexuals he was
sure, would love to see Terri Miller naked, and he was about to
have a front seat view of Terri's nakedness and all of her little
dirty secrets. He was sure she had some. Everyone did. He would
watch her until he decided when she would become his victim.
She would be his ultimate trophy. In the meantime, he would
feast his eyes and learn all the intimate details about
Jamaica's most famous law-officer. He hummed along to Kanye
West's new single *The Good Life*. Life was good indeed.

Roger went around to the general manager's office to let him
know that he was going to head up to Terri Miller's apartment to
do the installation. Patrick Gordon burst his bubble when he

informed him that it was already taken care of. Roger was disappointed. He was really looking forward to going up there. Terri was a bonafide celebrity and he had wanted to check out her apartment and perhaps get a glimpse of the mystery baby that everyone was talking about but few had actually seen. He wondered who was doing the installation but knew better than to ask. Patrick Gordon could be a real asshole sometimes. Maybe a relic from his days in the Police Force. After Roger left his office, Patrick wondered idly why his boss wanted to do this job himself. He didn't strike Patrick as the star-struck type, but then again Terri Miller was no ordinary woman.

Watson got to the apartment complex at 9:25. One of the two security guards approached his vehicle through the pedestrian gate, while the other remained in the booth. After stating his business, which the guard confirmed by buzzing the intercom at Terri's apartment, he was allowed to proceed. *You'd think the Prime Minister lives here,* he mused, as he parked in one of the two empty spots at apartment 7a. He looked around. There were fourteen apartments, seven on either side of the cul-de-sac. They were large, seemingly three bedroom units. Very upscale and attractive. Where he lived was nice too, but it was definitely a notch below this complex. That annoyed him. He shrugged his irritation aside and went up to the patio. The front door was open and the helper was standing there waiting. She was holding the cutest baby he had ever seen in her pudgy arms.

"Hi," he said to Mavis pleasantly. "Right on time?"

"Hello, yes you are," Mavis replied.

"Such a cute baby," he commented, as Mavis moved aside and allowed him to enter. "Your son?"

"No, this is my employer's child," Mavis told him, as she closed the front door. "Well, you know what to do so we'll get out of your way."

Watson could not stop staring at the baby, who had fixed him with an unsmiling, curious gaze. He had never seen grey eyes like that before. He knew it was ridiculous but the baby seemed to be staring in his soul. He turned away and opened his bag.

"Ok, I'll start out here first," he said to Mavis, referring to the patio.

"Ok," Mavis responded as she sat on the couch in the living room and played with Marc-Anthony. *Such a nice, powerfully built man*, she thought as she turned on the television. *Lovely American accent too*. It was on the cartoon network and Marc-Anthony grinned as SpongeBob and his friends appeared on the large 72 inch screen.

Watson installed the tiny but powerful wireless camera in the top right corner of the patio. He then went back inside and Mavis directed him to the baby's room. He liked Terri's home. It was exquisitely decorated: great ambiance; soft, soothing colours; expensive but understated furnishings; thick, luxurious carpeting throughout; exquisite artwork. He noticed that the apartment was decorated employing Feng Shui techniques. He wondered absently if she used a professional or did it herself. If it was the latter, she could have had a career in interior design.

He quickly set up the camera in the baby's room and after a quick glance to see if Mavis was still in the living room, he hurriedly stepped into Terri's bedroom. It was fit for a queen. However, he had no time to admire the room. He wasn't sure if Mavis knew that he was not supposed to be anywhere other than the baby's room and the living room area. He had wanted to put a camera in every single room in the apartment but it was better to play it safe. Her bedroom and bathroom was a *must* though. He screwed out the bulb in Terri's bedside lamp and replaced it with a special bulb that also functioned as a swivel camera. State of the art stuff that he gotten through his military contacts. He then hurried into Terri's lavish bathroom and placed two cameras in there. One in the toilet and another in the shower. Utter violation of the highest order. *Well not quite*, he grinned maliciously, *not quite*.

He went back out to the living room and installed the keypad for the alarm by the front door. He smiled at Mavis and asked her if he could use the kitchen counter for a few minutes. She waved sure and he placed his state of the art laptop on the kitchen counter and programmed all the devices. After he was through, he handed her a device which looked like a touch screen phone along with a charger, and told her that it was for her boss.

He declined Mavis' offer of coffee and Danish, and left. Mavis then called Terri to let her know that the technician had completed the installation and had left a device and some information for her.

Watson was extremely pleased with himself as he drove out of the complex. Later tonight when Terri Miller got home it was going to be show time. Lights, camera, action. Let the games begin.

Chapter 10

After the technician left, Mavis got herself and the baby ready to go on the road. She needed to go grocery shopping. Terri's favourite cereal was almost finished and they were low on several items. When they were ready to go, she informed Terri she was leaving the house and called Roderick, Terri's trusty cab driver. He had been referred to Terri by a cop whose judgment she trusted and when she had interviewed him, she had warmed to the fat, affable man who always had a merry twinkle in his eye. He was supposed to take Mavis and the baby on the road whenever Terri was busy. Roderick got there in ten minutes and he chatted with Mavis about current affairs until they arrived at Hosang's Supermarket, located in the upscale Barbican area. Mavis hated shopping there but that was where Terri instructed her to shop. Because of their location and clientele, their prices were higher than the average supermarket's. It just seemed like a waste of money. Mavis had to grudgingly admit though, that they were a class above the others in terms of stock, layout and ambience. She got herself one of the baby-friendly trolleys and Marc-Anthony shrieked with joy as she made her way over to the freshly baked products. There was a very attractive Hispanic-looking woman over there checking the expiry date on a loaf of wheat bread. Mavis pulled up alongside her and said hi as she reached for a pack of bagels. The woman responded pleasantly in a Spanish-sounding accent, and both women froze as they looked at the two baby boys who were suddenly playing with each other. They were practically identical.

Stunned, Maria's pretty face was twisted in consternation as she looked back and forth at Diego and the other child. *Dios Mio!* It couldn't be possible. Yet it was undeniable. Even if you were in denial about the stark resemblance, there were the eyes. Only one man had eyes like those. Anthony Garcia.

"Whose child is that?" Maria asked in a trembling voice, dismissing the possibility that the child belonged to the chubby, middle-aged woman standing beside her.

"Who are *you*?" Mavis demanded; trying to understand what was happening. Terri had told no one who fathered Marc-Anthony and it was painfully obvious that whoever the father was had also fathered a child with another woman. Should she tell Terri? Oh Lord. What a dilemma. She hated this damn supermarket even more now.

Maria threw down the bread and snatched Diego out of the trolley. She turned and walked away from Mavis without another word, leaving her trolley there with all the groceries she had already picked out. She didn't know what to do but she just couldn't stay there a moment longer. Diego had a brother! She wasn't the only one with whom Anthony had left a piece of himself. It was a disappointing discovery. She hurried out to the parking lot and placed a crying Diego in his car seat.

"*Pobrecita mi amor,*" Maria cooed as she strapped him in, kissing him on his forehead. "We need to go to a different supermarket so that mommy can think."

Maria then climbed into the Toyota Prado and headed out onto the main road. She turned left, deciding to go to one of the supermarkets in Liguanea. What was the right thing to have done? Should she have stayed and talked with the woman so that she could meet the mother of the child and see if the kids could grow up being aware of each other?

It had been a real shocker. She needed to clear her head. If it was meant to be, the brothers would meet again.

Terri got home at 7:30 that evening. Seeing as she expected the rapist to strike again the next day, she ensured she got home relatively early as there was no telling what was going to happen tomorrow. Mavis was in the kitchen with Marc-Anthony when she arrived.

"Hi Mavis," Terri said as she took Marc-Anthony from her arms and showered him with kisses. "How's my little prince? Did he miss his mommy?"

Mavis cleared her throat nervously. "Umm…this is the device the man left for you. Everything is set up but I didn't let him activate the alarm because you have to choose the password and stuff like that. See the manual and everything there on the counter. I'm going to lie down for a little while. Your supper is on the stove."

Terri looked at her. Mavis was not herself. Usually, she would have a bunch of questions about Terri's day and fill her in on anything that Marc-Anthony might have done that day. "Are you ok?"

"I'm fine Ms. Terri," Mavis replied, and kept on walking towards her room.

Terri followed. "Mavis…I know something is wrong. You're wound up tighter than that old grandfather clock you have on the wall. Now please, just tell me what the problem is."

Mavis sat on her bed and started to cry. She didn't want to tell Terri what she saw today. She knew it was going to hurt her. And the last thing she wanted was to be the bearer of bad news. Terri was very dear to her heart. She had never treated her with anything but love and respect.

Terri was truly alarmed now. Even Marc-Anthony had stopped smiling. Terri sat down beside Mavis.

"It's ok," Terri said soothingly. "Whatever it is we will deal with it. Just tell me."

Mavis started crying harder.

Terri waited.

"Marc-Anthony has a brother!" Mavis finally blurted out.

Terri looked at her as if she was the craziest person on the face of the earth.

Chapter 11

"How can that be?" Terri asked as calmly as she could. "What are you really saying Mavis?"

Mavis explained through her tears the strange scene at the supermarket. Terri listened without interrupting.

"Ovbiously you are mistaken Mavis," Terri said. A baby boy Marc-Anthony's age that looked just like him? Impossible.

"Is true Ms. Terri!" Mavis wailed. "Same pretty grey eye and everyt'ing. Even the other baby's mother was frightened. She run out leave her groceries right there like she see duppy!"

"Mavis…as I said, you *must* be mistaken. We will speak no further on the matter. Stop the crying and relax. Marc-Anthony has no brother. Ok? It was just one of those things I guess. You got caught up in the moment because of the woman's reaction. Babies tend to look like each other especially when they have the same complexion. I'm going to put Marc-Anthony to bed."

Terri got up and made her way to the baby's room. If what she said to Mavis was true why was her heart pounding so loudly? *I'm right,* Terri thought vehemently, trying her hardest to cast away any shred of doubt. *Marc-Anthony is an only child.*

Finally, **Watson said to himself excitedly, as Terri came into** view. He had been seated in front of the large screen in the control room since 7 p.m. He called Police Headquarters at 6:30 and asked to speak with Terri Miller. He had been told by the cop who answered the call that *Assistant Superintendent Miller* had left for the day, as if it was a crime to ask for the revered Terri Miller without prefacing her name with her title. Watson had hung up without saying thanks. He now watched as Terri walked around the room with the baby in her arms. He turned on the audio. She was singing a lullaby. Her voice was melodic. The lighting was poor as only a night lamp was on but that didn't diminish his excitement. There would be plenty of opportunities to see her in all her glory.

Marc-Anthony fell asleep in five minutes. Terri gently placed him in his crib, kissed him and made her way to her bedroom which was across from the baby's room. She closed the door behind her and switched on the bedside lamp. She shrugged off her blazer and removed the holster with her Glock 17 and hung it on the bed post. She then sat on the stool in front of her antique dresser and kicked off her Marc Jacobs boots. Terri stared at her reflection in the mirror as she released the bun and freed her hair. It was long and silky, reaching down to the middle of her back. Terri brushed her hair as she thought about what Mavis had told her. Usually, she trusted Mavis' judgment but not this time. She had to be wrong and that's all there was to it. There wasn't some woman out there walking around with Anthony's seed. Not her Anthony. Hell no.

Watson's breath did a sharp intake when Terri stood and pulled off her top. He leaned forward to the screen as she removed her jeans. He whistled appreciatively. Her underwear was a very sexy baby blue Victoria Secret number. The type of stuff women wore when they went on dates knowing they were going to get laid afterwards. That was the kind of stuff Terri Miller wore all the time apparently. God she was sexy. She showed no signs of having given birth. Her stomach was flat and her full breasts were still defying gravity. He gasped when she removed her bra and slipped off her panties. At that very moment, Carlton Watson was convinced that he was the luckiest man in Jamaica.

Terri took up her iPod and went into the bathroom to set her bath. Once the water was filled with soapy bubbles and at the right temperature, she slid in gracefully and sighed as she felt the day's stress seep out of her well-maintained body. She closed her eyes as she listened to the jazzy, soulful sounds of troubled British singer Amy Winehouse.

"Honey…are you ok?" Dr. Williams asked his wife as they relaxed in the living room. He had been home for an hour now and had quickly taken a shower and joined his wife in front of the TV where she had been watching the Home & Garden channel. The baby was sleeping and it was a cool, starry night. He was feeling randy. They had not made love in a little over a week and he was hoping to get some tonight. She seemed preoccupied though. He wondered what was eating her.

"I'm ok *mi esposo*," Maria replied warmly, in that accent he loved so much. He loved everything about the sensual Latina. From the moment he first laid eyes on her. He knew she thought that she was lucky to have him, but he knew that *he* was the lucky one. She had been through a lot and the way she had adjusted from the fast life to motherhood and family life was a testament to her strength and innate goodness. He had found true happiness with her and that, as far as he was concerned, was priceless. He didn't push though he knew something was bothering her. She would tell him when she was ready. She knew without a doubt that she could tell him anything.

Maria snuggled up closer to her husband. Though she could not get the incident at the supermarket out of her mind, she was aware that he was horny and was more than willing to fulfill her wifely duties. She spent the next twenty minutes pleasuring her husband on the comfortably worn leather couch. He was so caught up in rapture that he never even heard when she breathed Anthony's name.

Watson watched with baited breath as Terri prepared to climb out of the bath. He had never before seen a more appealing woman. She redefined sexy. He was so hard he thought he was going to pop a blood vessel. She stepped out of the bath and moved out of his line of vision. He cursed himself for not putting another camera in the bathroom. He wouldn't be able to see her again unless she used the toilet, and he would only get a brief shot. But what a shot it would be when she lowered herself to sit! He didn't think he could take it. He turned up the audio. Apparently she was drying herself and humming a tune he didn't recognize. She then returned to his line of vision when she sat on the bed and began to moisturize her naked body. He quickly grabbed his bottle of lube and started to masturbate furiously. When she bent over to slip on a pair of boy shorts he uttered a guttural roar and ejaculated all over himself. Breathing heavily, he suddenly felt angry. Furious in fact. The brief, intense explosion of pleasure had been replaced by discontentment and dissatisfaction. He looked down and felt disgusted at himself. He should be penetrating Terri Miller in every orifice until she begged for mercy, not spilling his seed on himself. Terri, sporting tiny shorts and a tank top, went back into the baby's room. She lifted him out of his crib and lay with him on the bed. Watson was thoughtful as he sat in his own fluids watching mother and son. If things ever got out of hand and he needed to get the upper hand on Terri Miller, he knew her Achilles heel. All he had to do was kidnap her son.

Chapter 12

Tormented and unfulfilled, Watson went into the bathroom to take a shower. He had gotten tired of watching Terri and the baby sleeping. *Cuddling with your baby at 9 p.m. on a Friday night, I think you need a life Ms. Miller*, he thought derisively as he selected an outfit to put on. He had decided to go hunting. The itch had become unbearable and he could not wait until Saturday to scratch it. *Change of plans.* It was a bit later than usual so he would have to improvise. He wouldn't catch any professional women leaving work at 9 p.m. on a Friday night. He would have to go somewhere where there was an after-work jam or something. He smiled at his reflection in the mirror. *You handsome fellow,* he mused. *Who could resist?*

Mavis got up out of bed at 9:30 to check on the baby. She stopped at the doorway when she saw mother and son sleeping on the bed. Mavis sighed. Poor Terri. Mavis knew that Terri chose not to believe her story because she would be too devastated by the truth. She hoped for Terri's sake they would never see that baby again but deep down she knew that would not be the case. What was in the dark always eventually came to light. Mavis turned away and returned to her room.

Watson opened the moon roof and put the windows down on his gleaming Range Rover Sport as he cruised New Kingston's hip strip. The strip was teeming with activity. Sexy women of all shapes and sizes were on the strip, heading to the different clubs and restaurants or just hanging out. He decided to park and go into Abe's lounge. He had been there once before and knew that it was a place where professionals liked to hang out after work. He scoped the parking lot as he parked. It was spacious and there were two guys out by the entrance. He figured he could snatch someone here easily enough if the opportunity presented itself. That wasn't necessarily the plan though. Hell, he didn't really have a plan. That could be dangerous as mistakes were most likely to be made then but who would make him pay? Terri Miller? *Please*. That bitch couldn't catch him even if he told her who he was. Chuckling, he made his way inside the lounge. The place was relatively packed when he went in. He smiled with the pretty host and told her he didn't require a table. He headed straight for the bar and took one of the few vacant seats at the corner where he had a decent enough view of the crowd.

He ordered the crabmeat on crackers and had a cold beer while he waited for his order. He looked around the room casually. He saw a woman that would be perfect. She was in a smart, expensively-tailored business suit with diamond earrings and a slender platinum bracelet. She also wore braces. *Probably a young lawyer or something like that* he thought. She was dining with two men though, and he figured the group would be leaving together. He finished his beer and his crabmeat still wasn't ready. He ordered another and looked up as a group of three young, stylish women walked in. The one that piqued his interest was the tallest and most voluptuous of the trio. Her hair was dyed blonde and cropped short. It suited her golden-brown complexion. They sat at a recently vacated table behind where he was sitting, and they were close enough for him to overhear bits and bobs of their conversation. He glanced at them discreetly through the mirror facing him at the bar. What he heard piqued his interest even more. It turned out the object of his interest was a lesbian. She was dating the short, petite one with the curly natural do and the third girl was a mutual friend. He would watch and see how things unfolded but there was no doubt about it, he was going to have that dyke for supper.

Chapter 13

erri woke up at 10:45 p.m. and placed Marc-Anthony back in his crib. She yawned and stretched and went into the kitchen to get something to eat. She had fallen asleep without eating and was now feeling ravenous. The supper that Mavis had prepared was still on the stove. She checked to see what it was. Barbequed chicken wings. Terri popped them in the microwave and poured a glass of fruit punch. Once the chicken was hot, she then placed two rolls on the plate and made her way to the living room where she turned to HBO. They were showing a replay of the Floyd Mayweather/Ricky Hatton fight. Though she had heard who won, she wanted to see how it all had unfolded. Terri was a big sports enthusiast. She had been very active herself in high school and university. She was on the swimming team in high school and had played lacrosse and tennis at university.

Watson was getting impatient. It was now close to 11 o' clock and the three women were still drinking and gossiping. How much longer did they plan to be there? He was rearing to go. The itch was becoming almost unbearable.

"You ok man?" The bartender asked. "Want another beer?"

Apparently his discomfort was showing on his face. *Not good.*

He attempted a smile. "Sure, one more for the road."

He had only taken two sips when he glanced in the mirror and realized that they were leaving. *Finally.* The object of his desire left some money on the table and the three women merrily made their way out of the lounge. He took another sip and left what he thought would cover his bill on the counter and quickly followed. Losing sight of them was not an option. He stood outside and pretended to check a message on his PDA as he watched the three women cross the street. One of them, the third wheel, got into a white Honda Civic that was parked on the side of road. They chatted for a few minutes then the two lovers waved bye and made their way to the parking lot.

Watson casually made his way across the street and followed them into the parking lot. He was hoping they had arrived in separate cars. If not, he would still find a way. He would not be deterred.

They did not. He reached his vehicle first and hopped in and watched as they stopped at a fire-engine red Honda Integra coupe, three cars away. He watched as the dyke pressed her girl-friend against the car and kissed her. They were giggling. He looked around the parking lot. There was no one around. He decided to make a move.

Terri had finished eating and was watching the fifth round of the exciting fight when Anna called.

"Hey girl," Anna said when Terri picked up. "Whatcha doin'?"

"I'm chilling, watching some boxing," Terri told her; knowing Anna was probably rolling her eyes.

She was.

"Ewww…anyways, I'm here…I think I'm staying in tonight," Anna told her. She was in bed naked watching the fashion channel. "I had a crazy night last night. I'm tired as hell."

"Ok, what did you do last night?" Terri asked, as she watched Mayweather land a powerful right hand to Hatton's jaw, staggering him. It was a miracle he was still on his feet.

"Have you heard of Reality X?"

"Yeah…I have." Terri replied. "I was invited to his launch. You went?"

"Yep…you were? You should've went girl…it was hype," Anna said.

"Hmmm," Terri grunted. She was always invited to all the big events but she rarely had the time or the desire to attend. Anna, on the other hand, was allergic to staying home.

"I hung out with Reality X after the launch…we went club hopping…popped ecstasy and fucked all night."

"Sounds like fun…" Terri commented sarcastically. Anna was something else.

"It was girl…but I need to rest up. Looking this beautiful requires a good night's sleep every now and then."

They chatted for awhile longer and after extracting a promise from Terri to hang out with her soon, Anna hung up. Terri wanted to pee but she had to wait until there was a break in the fight. It was so exciting she didn't want to miss anything.

Watson approached them quickly and stealthily, and before either of them realized what was happening, he had stepped up behind the tall woman and reached around with his handkerchief, clamping it over her nostrils while simultaneously holding a gleaming blade at the throat of her lover. The scream that she was getting ready to release immediately died in her throat. The tall woman slumped in his arms as the chloroform rendered her unconscious. Her lover watched him wide-eyed, her eyes begging him not to kill her as all the liquor she had consumed in the lounge ran down her short legs in a constant stream. *Casualties of war sweetheart,* he said to himself as he slashed her throat. He turned away as she fell to the ground, blood spraying from her neck like a hose. He walked quickly to his SUV and placed his prize in the passenger seat. He strapped on her seat belt and hopped in the vehicle. The Range Rover was heavily tinted so unless he was stopped by the cops and they searched the vehicle, no one would see her. He hoped he wasn't stopped though, as both he and the girl had been splattered by blood. That would be a little difficult to explain to the cops. The gate was open and there was now only one guy at the gate. He was sitting on a chair with his feet propped up, fast asleep. Good. One less complication to worry about. He turned up Trafalgar Road and put on his Otis Redding CD. He was feeling mellow.

When Watson was at the stoplight just 100 meters away from the parking lot, a group of four, two women and two men, were heading to their car when one of the women screamed when she saw the bloody body of a female lying on the ground. The other girl threw up repeatedly and one of the men ran back out to the street where he found two policemen standing outside of the police post located just two minutes away on Trinidad Terrace. They hurried back to the parking lot with him, one of them radioing in the reported discovery while he ran. Within five minutes there was a yellow police-line-do-not-cross tape around the crime scene and the strip was filled with cops. Terri got the call while she was watching the post game interview with the two fighters. She quickly got dressed in jeans, boots and a trendy leather jacket, and headed out to New Kingston.

Watson arrived at his complex in fifteen minutes. He pressed the button on the gate opener and waited impatiently for the electronic gate to open. The security guard at the gate peeped out through the window in his little booth and then went right back to his nap. Watson then opened his electronic garage door – he had paid a tidy sum for the developers to include this as none of the other apartments in the complex was built like that – and drove right in. Humming, he then removed the woman from the vehicle and carried her to the small room he called 'the lair'. Originally, the room – just behind the garage – was supposed to be the laundry room but he had other plans. He had told the contractor that it was going to be a home studio, so it wouldn't seem strange that he wanted the room to be sound-proof. He had removed the lone window and had installed the kind of bright lighting that was used in interrogation rooms.

He stripped the unconscious woman naked, marveling at her lush curves and body piercings. Wide childbearing hips; thick, toned legs; succulent golden-brown skin; large, firm breasts and a big juicy ass – a body designed for sin. He lightly ran his manicured fingers over her nipple rings, tugging them gently. He then kissed her labia, flicking the hoops she had in them back and forth with his tongue. He would enjoy ripping them all out later.

Chapter 14

There were several detectives at the crime scene when Terri arrived there. Even Stern, who was trying to act as if he was in charge. Terri ignored him and spoke to Detective Foster and the two cops who were first on the scene.

"Obviously she was hanging out somewhere on the strip and most likely she had not been alone," Terri said to him. "Have we checked around yet?"

"I've given her driver's license to one of the junior detectives to ask around at all the establishments within a two block radius. He's not back as yet."

Terri nodded her approval. Foster always did the right thing.

Terri looked at the body grimly. Such a waste.

Foster then got a call on his cell phone. He chatted briefly then hung up.

"That was the detective. He's asking us to come over to Abe's."

"Let's go," Terri said and they quickly made their way across the street. Stern looked on after them, wondering what had come up.

The detective led them around to the kitchen area of the restaurant where a young lady was waiting.

"Hi, I'm Assistant Superintendent Terri Miller and this is Detective Foster," Terri said, offering the frightened woman a handshake.

She shook Terri's hand and smiled weakly. *She's even prettier in person*, she thought, having seen Terri on TV several times.

"She recognized the girl," the junior detective was explaining. "She was the waitress that attended to their table."

"Ok, marvelous. Tell me everything you can remember," Terri urged with a disarming smile.

The waitress took a deep breath. She was nervous. She had never been questioned by the police before and she was shaken up at the news that the girl had been killed right across the street just after leaving there.

"Well…ummm…she came in with two other girls…and they were here for close to two hours…drinking and eating," she related. "They all left together a few minutes to 11."

"How was the bill paid and describe her companions," Terri said.

The waitress thought for a moment and then described the three women as best she could.

Foster scribbled some notes but Terri committed everything to memory. Terri thanked the waitress for her help and took her number just in case she needed to speak with her again. Terri examined the dead girl's driver's license. The address on it was a Kingston 6 address. Terri shook her head. Twenty years old. So sad. It was now 11:45 and a tad bit late but Terri decided to swing by the address and see if anyone was home. They needed to be notified and there was a possibility that they might know her friends. That would be a huge break.

"Foster, go back to the crime scene and make sure that everything has been taken care of. I'm going by this address to see if anyone is home," Terri told him. Foster nodded and he and the junior detective went back across the street. Terri hopped in her SUV and headed to Liguanea.

Watson's captive awakened at 12 midnight. She was disoriented momentarily, as her eyes adjusted to the unnaturally bright light. Her heartbeat accelerated as she looked around the room. What the fuck was going on? One minute she was kissing Eva in the parking lot and now she was naked and tied to a bed.

Nicole started crying as she screamed for help. She screamed until she was hoarse. After what seemed like an eternity – though only six minutes had elapsed since she woke up – the lone door to the room opened. Her eyes bulged in surprise. It was the loner from the bar who had been pretending not to watch them. Sweet Jesus. He was the rapist who had been terrorizing Kingston for the past week and a half! *Oh God! Why me?* Nicole thought in anguish.

"Please…my parents are rich…they'll give you anything you want…just don't hurt me…" Nicole implored.

Watson stepped over to the bed quickly and administered a hard back-handed slap to her face. Nicole cried out in pain.

"I don't need your fucking charity," Watson growled contemptuously. "Money can't buy everything… you rich spoilt bitch. No amount of money in the world can spare you from your fate."

"You fucking sick, weak, evil bastard," Nicole spat defiantly. "Going around hurting innocent women…battyman!"

Oh. No. She. Did. Not. Just. Call. Him. A. Faggot.

Watson slapped her again. And again. And again. She was dizzy by the time he ceased.

"You're going to beg me to kill you by the time I'm through with you," he promised solemnly. He removed his robe. He was naked underneath. She averted her eyes from his tattooed torso and burgeoning erection. Her body went into shut down mode as she resigned herself to her terrible fate.

Watson climbed on the bed and positioned himself between her legs. He would no longer use condoms. His power was growing. No one could stop him. He entered her with a brutal thrust. Nicole grunted despite her best efforts and raised her head slightly and spat in his face. He stopped moving long enough to wipe her saliva with his fingers which he then placed in his mouth.

Nicole almost puked.

Watson thought of Terri Miller as he fucked her as hard as he could. He reached down and ripped the two hoops from her fleshy labia as he ejaculated inside her. Nicole released a gut-wrenching scream that warmed his heart.

Chapter 15

Terri arrived at the complex in Liguanea Plains and honked her horn lightly at the massive electronic gate. The security guard came out through the pedestrian entrance to speak with her.

"Yes Ma'am?" he queried politely, wondering where he had seen the gorgeous face looking at him before.

"Hi, I'm Assistant Superintendent Terri Miller," she told him. "I need to speak with the occupants of Apartment 6 as a matter of urgency."

Rassclaaat! That's who she is! The guard thought excitedly. He excused himself and went into the booth to buzz Dr. Hines. The good doctor would not be pleased at being disturbed this hour in the morning.

"Hello?" Dr. Hines said groggily. He absolutely *hated* when someone woke him up. He had heard the intercom buzzing but had tried to ignore it or let his wife get it but she was dead to the world.

"Sorry to wake you Doc, this is Smithy at the gate," the guard said. "Assistant Superintendent Terri Miller is here to see you and she says it's very urgent."

That got Dr. Hines wide awake. *Oh God! Did the mother really report it? How was he supposed to know she was under-aged? Sweet Jesus no! He had paid her what she wanted. That wicked, conniving woman!*

Dr. Hines cleared his throat. "Did she say what she wanted?" he asked, though he knew it was a stupid question. Why would the Assistant Superintendent of Police divulge anything to the security guard?

"No, Sir," the guard responded.

The doctor sighed. "Send her in."

He went into the bedroom to get his robe. *God please let it be something else,* he prayed. *I promise I'll be faithful from now on.*

Both parking spots in front of the apartment were filled so Terri parked behind the white Mercedes. She got out quickly and walked up to the patio. The doctor opened the door and invited her in.

"I'm so sorry to disturb you," Terri began, "but I'm afraid I have bad news."

"Do I need a lawyer?" Dr. Hines asked.

Terri frowned. Why would he ask her that? And why was he wearing out the rug? "No, you don't. I think you need to sit though."

Dr. Hines was relieved as he sat down. Ovbiously that wicked woman hadn't gone to the police. He sat and crossed his legs and smugly waited for Terri to continue.

"Are you related to Eva Hines?" Terri asked softly.

The smug expression on Dr. Hines' face vanished. Was his princess in trouble?

"I'm her father…" he replied cautiously.

"There's no easy way to tell you this…so I'm just going to go ahead and say it. Eva, your daughter, was murdered tonight."

"Oh God no!" Dr. Hines cried out clutching his heart.

"Claude?" a woman's voice called out from somewhere inside the apartment as Terri quickly called Foster.

"Get an ambulance to Apartment 6 at Liguanea Plains apartment complex now!" Terri instructed. She hung up without explaining anything further. She went over to Dr. Hines and held him as he went into cardiac arrest.

"What the hell is going on out here?" the woman demanded when she came out to the living room. "Jesus Christ! What have you done to my husband? Claude! Lord have mercy!"

Terri tried to calm her down but to no avail. She prayed the ambulance got there quickly.

Watson stood naked in front of the full length mirror in his spacious bathroom. The itch had been scratched. He felt powerful and satisfied. He had kept his promise. She had indeed begged him to kill her. Anything to stop the pain and the horror. She had fainted after he had amputated her right leg. He had revived her before cutting off the left. Soon it would be Terri Miller's turn. But all in due time. He went into the shower to cleanse himself. He had made quite a mess carving up his unwilling guest.

Terri leaned against her BMW X5. She was outside the Hines' apartment. She was emotionally and physically drained. She could still hear the ambulance sirens in the distance as it raced to the nearest hospital carrying both husband and wife. The wife had suffered a stroke when she realized that her husband was having a heart attack. She didn't even know about her daughter yet. *What a night*, Terri mused ruefully. She had never experienced anything like it. Foster was silent as he watched her. He had accompanied the ambulance with back-up as he hadn't known if Terri was in trouble.

Watson was in the shower singing when he heard the sirens. What the hell? Impossible! His heart pounding, he wrapped himself in a towel and went by the window. He did not turn on the living room light. He watched as two attendants carefully wheeled two gurneys into the back of the ambulance. The old couple next door. He wondered what had happened. He tensed when he saw Terri Miller exit the apartment and lean against a black SUV. *So close.* He started to itch immediately. The bitch was really under his skin. He couldn't even look at her without getting agitated. He watched as she waved bye to three cops and they drove off leaving her still standing by her vehicle. She looked tired and stressed. He chuckled. *Keep your chin up, Super-cop, Jamaica is depending on you.* He watched her until she got in her vehicle and drove away. He memorized her license plate. He then went back into the bathroom to complete his shower.

Terri sighed as she exited the complex. She was drop dead tired. She would go home and get a few hours sleep before going to the hospital to check on the Hines'. She hoped that the identities of the other two girls would be ascertained soon. Best case scenario, they would hear about their friend's death and come to the police with any information they might have. Terri turned on the CD player and selected Lauryn Hill's classic album. She hummed the lyrics to *Everything is Everything* and tried to relax her mind. She couldn't wait to get home and jump in bed. She just knew that in a few hours she was going to have a long day. She could never have imagined just how long and crazy it was going to be.

Chapter 16

Latoya woke up at 7:15 a.m. Saturday morning. She checked the time, groaned and crawled out of bed to go to the bathroom. After leaving the girls last night, she had stopped by her boyfriend for a quickie before heading home. Normally she would have spent the night but she was going to Fort Lauderdale with her mother to attend her aunt's wedding. The flight was 10 a.m. which meant that they needed to get to the airport by the latest 8:45. She was in the shower when her mom peeped in her room to see if her notoriously late daughter had gotten up. Latoya showered quickly, got dressed and joined her mom in the kitchen for a quick breakfast. The 8 a.m. news was on the radio. They listened attentively as the reporter started with news of the brutal murder of a twenty year old woman in the JIK parking lot last night in New Kingston. Latoya choked on her scrambled eggs when she heard the name.

"Lord have mercy!" her mother cried. "*Your* friend Eva?"

Latoya ran to the bathroom to throw up. They didn't make the flight to Miami.

Terri went to the Caribbean University Hospital to check on the status of the Hines' at eight Saturday morning. Dr. Hines had survived the heart attack and was in a relatively stable condition but his wife was experiencing post-stroke spasticity – muscle tightness that impairs mobility. The doctors were careful not to let her learn of her daughter's demise just yet. They feared the news would kill her. Terri received a call on her mobile as she left the hospital. Apparently someone had called headquarters claiming to be the mother of one of the girls that had been with the murder victim the night she was killed. She had insisted that she would speak with no one but Terri Miller and had left a number for Terri to call her back. Terri memorized the number and dialed it quickly as she slowly exited the hospital grounds.

"Hello," said a weary sounding voice.

"Ms. Moore? This is Terri Miller," Terri said.

"Ms. Miller, thanks for returning my call so promptly," Ms. Moore intoned, "my daughter was a good friend of the deceased and she was with her the night she…"

Ms. Moore broke down in tears. Terri could hear more crying in the background. That must be the daughter. Apparently they had been really close.

Terri waited until Ms. Moore composed herself enough to continue speaking.

"It's not a good time to talk obviously but I can imagine you need all the information you can get as soon as possible…" Ms. Moore said, sniffling. "So come and see us now if you can."

"Thank you Ms. Moore, and I really appreciate this," Terri said sincerely, "I'll be there in a few minutes."

Ms. Moore gave her the address and Terri headed there as quickly as she could.

Terri arrived at the house, located at Tucker Avenue, in fourteen minutes. Terri drove through the open gate and parked at the front of the spacious yard, next to a silver Mercedes station wagon. It appeared that Ms. Moore was well off. Tucker Avenue used to be *the* address to have back in the day, and though it had lost some of its prominence, it was still a very decent neighbourhood. A puffy-faced, teary-eyed Ms. Moore greeted her at the door.

Terri hugged her and Ms. Moore led her inside. The daughter, Latoya, was curled up on the lovely beige sofa, crying softly.

Terri gently spoke with her for the next twenty minutes and after getting all the information she could from the heartbroken young woman, she again thanked them both profusely and left. She was thoughtful as she exited the premises and headed to the address that Latoya had provided for Nicole Boorasingh, the *girl-friend* of the deceased. Latoya had told Terri that she was unable to reach Nicole, numerous calls to all her numbers went unanswered and her parents had not heard from her since earlier the previous day. Terri's gut feeling was that there would be more grief. Based on what Latoya told her, the three girls had left the lounge together and then Latoya had driven off first seeing as she had gotten a park on the curb and she was going to a different destination. The other two girls had driven in the same car, and would be going by Nicole's apartment for the night. That meant that Nicole had been with Eva when she was killed. Did the killer kidnap her? And why? If it was a robbery why was Eva's pocketbook with her credit cards and money left untouched? Why didn't he take her jewellery? Terri sighed with dread. She was certain that the rapist had struck again. Eva was probably killed because she was in the way. The rapist was getting unpredictable, changing his pattern. But why? What did that signify? Was he trying to throw off the scent? Or was he getting out of control? Terri's phone then rang. The call made her detour to police headquarters.

Chapter 17

Her heart heavy with dread, Terri swung into her reserved parking space at Police Headquarters. She parked quickly and walked with long strides into the building. The Commissioner and Detective Foster, and the cop who had gotten the delivery, were waiting for her on the eleventh floor. Detective Foster had called Terri informing her that a large box had been delivered there with a sealed envelope addressed to Assistant Superintendent Terri Miller. URGENT! IMPORTANT! had been labeled all over the box and the return address read: Wolf Man c/o Horror Gardens, Kingston 4. Terri had instantly known it was from him. She had told Foster to take the package and the cop who received it to the conference room and ask the Commissioner to meet her there. She would soon find out if she was right. If she was, she had a very good idea what was in that box.

Carlton Watson felt invincible as he stepped out of the cab and made his way to where he had parked his vehicle. He had left it in the parking lot of the supermarket where he shopped which was in the New Kingston area and only about 10 minutes away from Police Headquarters. He, the most wanted and feared man in Jamaica - especially after the public knows that he was responsible for the latest two murders - had walked into the lobby and dropped off a package containing the head, legs, and arms of the woman he had raped and killed last night to the cop on duty. He hadn't even worn a disguise, just a cap and a pair of large, over-sized Prada sunglasses. He knew they would have kept his delivery from the press, so he had sent a copy of the note and a description of the contents of the box to an investigative reporter at The Gleaner. Based on what he had heard, this particular reporter lived for the limelight and would have no qualms to make it public even if the police refused to confirm it. The public deserved to know the full extent of the *Wolf Man's* wrath. Damn he loved his self-prescribed moniker. Had a nice ring to it. He hummed as he went inside the supermarket to pick up a few items. He felt for a big lunch of mashed potatoes, dumplings and calalloo with saltfish.

The look on everyone's face was grim as Terri, having slipped on a pair of latex gloves, opened the envelope attached to the box. The hand-written note read:

Hi Terri,

We are already acquainted (don't get sleepless nights trying to figure out how) but I will formally introduce myself. I am the Wolf Man. When we meet in an intimate setting, you will see why I chose that moniker. Cute aint it? Anyhow, until we meet, kindly step up your pathetic investigative efforts. Obviously you won't be able to catch me but at least make it interesting. Cute son by the way, it would be a shame if anything should happen to him. See you soon sexy. Now get to work. Hope you like the gift.

Yours truly,

The Wolf Man

Terri took deep long breaths and forced herself to remain calm. The opposite of what he wanted, she was sure. He was trying to get to her head but he would soon find out just who he was messing with. There was no doubt in her mind that she was going to hunt him down and kill him like the animal he undoubtedly was. Her face was stoic as she wordlessly handed the note to the Commissioner. She then turned her attention to the box. She used a box cutter to remove the strong tape and opened it. The young cop, who had received the package at the front desk in the lobby, covered his mouth as if to suppress either a scream or vomit. Terri lifted the head out of the box. It was obvious that the woman had died screaming. *Jesus Christ*...someone swore in a strained whisper behind her. The bastard had beheaded her while she was still alive. At that moment, Terri knew sleep would not come easy until she caught this depraved, psychotic murderer.

"Take everything down to forensics for an analysis," Terri instructed to Foster. "I need the note to be checked by a hand-writing expert. Use Mrs. West. She's the best in the island." She then turned to the cop who had received the package.

"Report to my office now," Terri told him. She needed to know everything he remembered about receiving it. She had a hunch that the bastard was cocky enough to bring it here himself. She told the Commissioner she would update him later that day and then went up to her office with the nervous young cop in tow. He felt sick to his stomach. Suppose it was the killer himself that had brought the package? The Police Force would be the laughing stock of the entire country, and he would be the scourge of his peers.

"Try to relax and tell me everything you remember," Terri said soothingly, knowing that the poor man was distraught. He wasn't to blame though. He had no way of knowing that the most wanted man in Jamaica would come into Police Headquarters to make a delivery. When the public and the media heard about it though, Terri was sure they wouldn't look at it so rationally.

He recounted what he remembered as best he could and Terri mercifully told him to go home for the remainder of the day.

She was pensive as she stared at the lovely view her office provided. This guy was of the caliber of infamous psychos that had emerged in the US over the years. He would have been as notorious as any of them had he been there. She thought of the return address on the envelope. *Horror Gardens.* The sick bastard's idea of a joke, Terri thought. *Kingston 4.* Number of victims so far? Probably. She read the handwritten note over in her mind. Something was nagging her. There was something she was not picking up on. *Cute aint it?* That was how some black Americans spoke. So he was either someone who traveled to the states frequently, used to live there or was just one of those Jamaicans who loved to adopt all things American. Maybe it was nothing, but her instinct told her it was an important observation. Also, what did he mean by *we are already acquainted*? The man the cop had described was wearing large sunglasses and a cap that had effectively covered his face, but physically, he fit Terri's profile to a T: well-built, tall and athletic. He had referred to her as sexy and intimated that he would *see her soon.* Terri got up and paced the room. *He desired her.* He considered her an eventual victim. *Well,* Terri surmised just as her extension rang, *I will have to make it be sooner than later. Tease the bastard into coming for me before he's ready.* She answered the beep. Her secretary told her that Mitch Constantine from The Gleaner was on the line. Terri wondered what the irresponsible, persistent, immoral, poor excuse for a journalist wanted. The man was despicable. He would do anything for a sensational headline. *Anything* to sell papers. She took the call.

"Ms. Miller," he drawled, in that annoyingly smug tone he had employed ever since he had become one of the island's most well-known journalists. "How are you this afternoon? Feeling the pressure I might imagine?"

"How can I help you Constantine?" Terri asked abruptly, not masking the displeasure in her voice.

Constantine chuckled. "Testy aren't we...would that have anything to do with that package that was delivered to your office today by *The WolfMan?*"

How the fuck did he find out? Terri thought in despair. She could just see the headlines now. *Fucking asshole.*

"I haven't a clue what you're babbling about Constantine and be warned, if you print any fabrications from your deranged mind as fact, action will be taken up against you and The Gleaner."

Constantine laughed. "You can deny it all you want but the public has a right to know what's going on and as a reporter, it's my sworn duty to inform them. Make sure you read the papers tomorrow. It's going to be a screamer."

Terri hung up the phone and immediately looked in her address book for the number of the Managing Director of The Gleaner. He played golf with her dad most Sundays, and was a family friend. Terri got him on his mobile.

"Hello," he intoned, sounding harried.

"Hi Mr. Bryce, its Terri Miller," Terri said. "How are you?"

"Hi there...I'm ok, having a shitty day at the office but what else is new," he replied, pausing to light his cigar. "How is everything going? Soon catch that bastard? Martha is scared to death."

They both chuckled. His wife, a sweet lady who loved plants like they were people, was sixty years old.

"Listen...usually I wouldn't ask you to interfere but somehow, one of your reporters, Constantine to be exact, has gotten hold of sensitive information about the case...really nasty stuff... and is going to press with it. I'd like for you to kill the story."

Harold Bryce puffed his cigar. Constantine had already come to him with the story and he had approved it. They knew how to swing stories like this. And Ms. Miller knew that too, despite her threats to Constantine about litigation.

"I can't do that Terri," Bryce told her. He figured tomorrow's edition would be completely sold out island-wide by 12 noon.

The story was incredible. "It would go against my morals. My job is to provide the public with news, however unsavoury that news might be."

"Thank you for your time, and enjoy the rest of your day," Terri said politely as she terminated the call. She sighed and looked at the time. It was 1:30 p.m. Though she didn't have much of an appetite she knew she should eat. Her parents usually visited Marc-Anthony on a Saturday and Sunday, and they were probably at her house now. She looked on her desk for the mobile device that was linked to the cameras she had installed at the house but it appeared she had left it in the car. She hadn't spoken to them for a few days now. The relationship was still a bit strained, especially from her end. She knew she needed to forgive them for the way they had acted when she was pregnant, but the wound was slow to heal. She needed to get in touch with the parents of the latest victim to let them know what had happened to their daughter. The father was a well-known businessman and the mother a popular socialite. Terri had their numbers and knew where they lived but she decided to go home and take a short break before tackling the unpleasant task.

Chapter 18

Mavis was able to spend some time cleaning the apartment as Marc-Anthony's grandparents had come to visit and were happily playing with their grandson. She was cleaning the toilet in Terri's bathroom when she noticed the small object. She dipped her gloved-hand in and extracted it. She wasn't sure what the eye-looking object was but she was certain it hadn't been there last Saturday when she had cleaned this bathroom. She placed it in a small plastic bag so she could ask Terri about it when she came home.

Watson watched the happenings in the office as he ate the large lunch he had prepared. The office was open on Saturdays, but they closed an hour earlier than usual. Nothing much was happening. He knew Terri wasn't home so he didn't bother to check her cameras. He slipped in the DVD of his most recent victim. It was fast becoming his favourite. This would be his third viewing already. The look on the young woman's face when he was about to decapitate her lovely head was priceless.

Terri changed her mind and decided to take care of business
before going home for lunch. It wasn't right for her to put off
notifying the girl's parents. She headed up to Jacks Hill where
they resided. Though the entire area was affluent, the mansion
was located at the end of a street known to be the most exclusive
section in Jacks Hill. Terri conferred with the guard at the gate
and was allowed to proceed. A maid greeted her at the door and
took her to see Mrs. Boorasingh who was entertaining friends at
the poolside. Mrs. Boorasingh excused herself from the small,
intimate gathering of bikini clad, champagne-guzzling women
and came over to speak with the celebrated cop in private.

"Hi, nice to meet you," she said pleasantly, though rather
loudly, to Terri. "I think you're so fabulous. So what brings you
to my humble abode?"

Terri smiled her thanks, noting the glaze in the woman's eyes
and her unnaturally high-pitched voice. The woman was high. Terri
had been invited to several parties here but had never attended.
Mrs. Boorasingh tactfully did not bring that up.

Terri cleared her throat. "There's no easy way for me to tell
you this but something terrible has happened to your daughter,
Nicole."

Mrs. Boorasingh's smile remained intact. She waited for Terri
to continue.

"She was killed last night," Terri said softly.

"I see," Mrs. Boorasingh said nonchalantly, as if Terri had
commented on the weather as opposed to telling her that her child
was dead. "Thank you for coming by."

Terri nodded sympathetically and turned away. Apparently
she had just taken a strong hit of cocaine. Her brain was too numb
to really process the information she had just received. Terri had
noticed the white powder on the small glass table where the
ladies were seated. She shook her head as she hopped in her SUV.
Well at least it hadn't been as dramatic a scene as what happened
at the Hines'. She waved bye to the security guard and hoped for
Mrs. Boorasingh's sake that she was still high when she heard
the circumstances surrounding her daughter's death.

"Hi, mom, dad," Terri said when she got home and entered the living room. Marc-Anthony grinned when he saw his mother. Terri scooped him from off his grandfather's knees.

"You love your mommy don't you...hmmm...my little prince," Terri cooed, throwing him up in the air as he squealed with delight. He loved the rough play.

"Hi honey," her father responded. "How is everything going?"

"It's very hectic right now but I'm ok," Terri told him.

"Your aunt Mabel will be coming to Jamaica on Monday," her mother advised, though she was sure Terri already knew. Mabel had probably called her first.

"Yeah, she told me," Terri said. Mabel was her favourite aunt. She was the youngest of her mother's four sisters and was a real sweetheart. She was only twelve years older than Terri so they had always been close. Mabel had called her a week ago to let her know that she would be visiting for a few days.

Terri drifted to the kitchen with Marc-Anthony to see what Mavis had prepared for lunch. Grilled chicken sandwiches and cole slaw. She fixed herself a plate and sat at the kitchen counter to eat. She made small talk with her parents until she was through then handed Marc-Anthony to his grandmother and went into her room. Mavis, who had been cleaning the baby's room, called out to her.

"Ms. Terri, just a minute please," she said.

Terri peeked in.

"I found this in your toilet, thought I'd show it to you," Mavis said, handing her the small plastic bag. "I didn't see it in there last time I cleaned so I was wondering if it's something that you had put there and if I should fasten it back in the bowl."

Frowning, Terri took the bag with the tiny object from her. She thanked Mavis and went into her bathroom. She quickly slipped on a pair of latex gloves and removed the object from the bag. Terri examined it carefully. She wasn't a hundred percent sure but it seemed to be either a camera or a tracking device. Either way what the fuck was it doing in her toilet? Mavis said it hadn't been there when she last cleaned which was a week ago. Apart from her parents today, no one had been in the house except for the technician from POW Electronics. Terri's head was spinning. Why would the technician install a device in her toilet? Were there other devices in the house? *Fucking hell!* Terri thought. *This is serious.* She looked at the device again. Really high-tech. Whatever it was. She whipped out her mobile to call David. He was the resident techie in the forensics department. David devoured technology magazines the way most men devoured porn. He answered on the first ring.

"Superintendent Miller," he chirped. He never said assistant. As far as David was concerned, Terri Miller was the boss. "What's up?"

Terri smiled. She could see him now, hunched over a PC, spectacles on his nose, lusting over the latest electronic gadgets on the internet.

"Hi David," Terri said. "I have a device here that I need you to take a look at for me. Are you in the lab?"

"Yeah," David replied.

"Ok, I'll be there in a little while," Terri told him and hung up. Once she knew for sure what the device was, someone at POW Electronics would have a lot of explaining to do. She also needed to 'sweep' the apartment to see if there were any other hidden devices in the apartment. There was only one such device in the Police Force – a gift from Scotland Yard. She would get the device which was stored in an area where only cops with the highest level of authority could access, and come back with David after he looked at what she had found.

After kissing her son and saying goodbye to her parents, Terri quickly made her way down to Police Headquarters. She needed to get to the bottom of this and fast.

Chapter 19

After eating and watching the DVD of the last attack he had carried out, Watson became cognizant of the fact that he was no longer in control of the beast. No longer could he wait a few days to scratch the itch. The need to dominate, conquer and kill was becoming constant now, the thirst only quenchable for a few hours. Despite the immense enjoyment of the last experience, he was already rearing to go a mere few hours later. Terri Miller had become a constant presence on his mind. The hunter was about to become the hunted. He would capture her soon and take her to his lair. He would keep her captive for seven days, before painfully snuffing out her existence, so he could savour every drop of what he was positive would be his most fulfilling experience yet, ranking right up there with his mother's death twenty years ago. Watson smiled at the memory of his mother's demise as he grabbed his keys and headed out to his SUV. It used to produce conflicting emotions in the early days, but the pleasure of the act had vastly outweighed any remorse he might have felt about taking the life that had given him life. She had definitely had it coming.

Watson reminisced on the day he had murdered his mother as he drove out to New Kingston. He wasn't sure what he had in mind once he got there, but he was confident the right opportunity would present itself. Following on the heels of his discovery that his mother was a prostitute, was the revelation that she was also a drug addict. Her increased drug use led to the deterioration of her appearance and as such, she didn't attract as much clientele as she used to. The quality of her clientele had also dipped significantly; she only attracted the real dregs of society who would sometimes barter drugs with her in exchange for the vilest and most degrading sexual acts. One Saturday morning, as young Carlton lay hungry in his bed after waking up and venturing out to the kitchen to find the cupboards and the kitchen bare, one of his mother's customers, a tall, well-built Caucasian man who would have sex with anything as long as it breathed, had come into his room and had his way with him after giving his mother a twenty-dollar bag of cocaine and a Big Mac. The pain had been unbearable and not once, during the horrific twenty minutes, when he had screamed until he was hoarse, did his mother even glance into the room. She never mentioned the incident and it became a regular occurrence – occurring at least once a week, sometimes with different men. It continued for three months and on his tenth birthday, young Carlton entered his mother's bedroom in the wee hours of the morning and climbed on top of her naked, sleeping form in the filthy bed. She had awakened from her drug-induced haze, her blood-red eyes bulging in shock to see her son astride her holding a large kitchen knife at her scrawny neck.

"What the fuck are you doing Carlton?" she had asked angrily. "Have you lost your fucking mind just like your worthless daddy?"

Carlton's father, whom he never met, had lost his mind and was committed to the asylum when his mother was seven months pregnant with him, back when she still resided in Jamaica. The cause of his mental illness was never ascertained.

"Taking you out of your misery," Carlton had whispered as he slit her throat. He had then stabbed her dead, nude body until his hands were tired. Exhilarated, he had then calmly hid the murder weapon and called 911, tearfully telling the police that one of his mother's customers had murdered her and fled the scene. The police had arrived to find him sobbing and in a state of shock, lying in a pool of blood next to his mother. Hours later, in an interview with a child psychologist and several detectives, he tearfully told them about hiding when he heard the screams but that he had recognized the man's voice as he was a regular customer. He described the man who had first raped him as the murderer. The police, after showing a sketch of the suspect around the neighbourhood, picked up the man at a construction site where he was working. The man eventually was found guilty of first degree murder based on Carlton's testimony and his inability to come up with a credible alibi that he was home alone sleeping at the time of the murder, and was sentenced to sixty years in prison, which at the age of 39, was a life sentence. Young Carlton became a ward of the state, and after bouncing around in various foster homes, joined the army the day after he turned eighteen.

Watson stopped at the Esso gas station on Knutsford Boulevard when he got to New Kingston. He told the attendant to fill up the tank and casually glanced at the car at the pump next to him. It was a pearl white Lexus coupe. It was driven by the tall, exotic-looking woman he had seen at Reality X's album launch a couple days ago. He smiled. Today was not her lucky day.

Chapter 20

"It's definitely a camera," David stated. "Wow...this is really advanced stuff...not yet on the market and won't be for some time yet."

Terri was extremely angry though her face remained stoic. She had not told David that the camera had been in her toilet. It was too embarrassing. She felt so violated. She took the camera back from David and slipped it in the pocket of her blazer.

"Let's go to my apartment to do a sweep," Terri told him. "Drive your own vehicle as I won't be coming back here immediately. I have a very important stop to make."

"Ok," David said as he shut down his laptop.

Terri's mind was churning. Did this have anything to do with the case? Or was it just the action of a perverted mind trying to get his kicks? Either way, somebody was in big trouble.

They got to Terri's apartment five minutes apart. Her grandparents were still there. They swept the patio first and the only camera there was the one that Terri had ordered. Terri then asked everyone to sit on the patio for awhile and she and David painstakingly swept the entire apartment. They located the presence of five cameras in total. Terri had only ordered two to be installed.

Someone had been watching her in some of her most intimate moments for the past four days. She could not recall having been angrier in her life than she was at that very moment. Then something clicked. *We're already acquainted…* wasn't that what the psycho calling himself the *Wolf Man* said? It couldn't be. Terri trembled at the thought that she just might have gotten a lead on the sick bastard. It was a long shot but she had learnt a long time ago to trust her instincts. And right now they were telling her that he had something to do with this. She trembled at the thought that the *Wolf Man* had been in her home.

"David, I have to go," Terri told him. "Thanks for your help."

"No problem," David replied. "Do you want me to take this stuff down?"

He was still amazed at the high-tech gadgets they had found in the Assistant Superintendent's apartment. Someone had been watching her and based on where the cameras were located, had seen her in all her glory. Who could possibly have access to all this high-tech stuff that was not commercially available?

"No, its ok…I'll take them down to Headquarters when I'm ready," Terri told him. "Not a word of this to anyone David."

"My lips are sealed," David replied.

Terri knew she could trust him which was why she brought him up here with her in the first place - along with his technical expertise - but due to the fact that this could potentially be a big break, she wanted to officially tell him to keep it under wraps.

Terri left the apartment quickly and made her way to Half-Way-Tree. Time to pay POW Electronics a visit.

Chapter 21

Watson got out of his SUV and walked over to the woman's car. She was sending an email on her Palm Treo and looked up when he came to her window.

"Hi," Watson said to her, flashing his colgate smile. "I'm Carlton."

Anna shook his hand.

"I'm Anna."

"I just had to come over and say hi…I saw you the other day at an album launch…where in God's name did you get that outfit? You gave every man in the room an erection."

Anna was mildly shocked at his boldness. Most men were not that forward. She liked that. She examined him more closely. He was good looking with a very nice body. He was powerfully built without looking too bulky. Manicured hands. Rolex watch. American accent. Range Rover Sport. Not bad at all.

Anna chuckled and licked her lips provocatively.

"Is that right?"

"So where are you headed?" Watson asked. "Can I take you to an early dinner?"

Anna thought for a brief moment. She was about to head over to the modeling agency to hang out with the girls for a bit. Her friend, April, had just returned from doing the Gucci show in London and had asked Anna to swing by. Well she didn't have to go now. The agency was located in a complex that housed a bar, restaurant and a gym, all owned by the head of the agency, so Anna knew that they would be there for awhile. She could have dinner with this guy. See what he was all about.

The attendant called out to Watson and he paid her for the gas in cash. He turned back his attention to Anna.

"So...are you game?"

"Ok, where did you have in mind?" Anna asked.

"How about that new Indian joint on Braemar Road? I hear the chicken tikka masala is excellent."

Anna liked his style.

"Sounds good to me," she purred. "Lead the way."

Anna drove behind Watson and they arrived at the restaurant in ten minutes. They parked beside each other. Watson admired her long, toned legs as she exited the vehicle. *Self- centered, materialistic slut*, he thought as he looked at her clothing. Christian Dior plaid shorts, white Gucci baby T and Emilio Pucci loafers.

Anna saw the lust in his eyes. No surprise there. Anna considered herself to be the hottest thing smoking. Only Terri, in her estimation, could compare. They went inside the restaurant and there was a fairly decent crowd there enjoying an early Saturday evening dinner. It was now 4 p.m. Watson led the way inside and the host directed them to a table for two close to the back of the restaurant.

Anna allowed him to order the dish he had recommended, and they chatted while they waited.

"So what do you do?" Watson asked.

"Oh, I'm one of the top models from Jamaica," Anna said airily. "I've worked with all the top designers and photographers."

"That's impressive...I'm in esteemed company..." Watson commented.

"You better believe it Mister," Anna said with a grin.

I'm going to enjoy carving up this narcissistic bitch, Watson thought as he smiled at her.

Anna loved to talk and Watson relaxed in his chair as she told him about her fabulous life. His interest piqued when she mentioned that her best friend was the best and brightest cop the Jamaica Police Force had ever seen. Watson leaned forward.

"Really, that's interesting," he said. "What's his name?"

"It's a her. Terri. Terri Miller. We've been best friends since high school," Anna told him. "So where are you from?"

"New Jersey," Watson replied absently. His mind was churning. Terri Miller. Their paths were definitely intertwined. What were the odds that this boring cunt would be someone dear to Terri Miller? He wondered how hard Terri would take it when he sent Anna's remains to her tomorrow. If what this garrulous bitch said was true, Terri would be devastated. The evening had just gotten very interesting. He thought of the best way to get Anna to come home with him. Brute force probably wouldn't be necessary. She definitely seemed like she would be up for an adventurous evening. All the blood in his body seemed to accumulate in his loins as he thought of how shocked and scared she would be when she discovered that she had entered a world of unspeakable horrors. He smiled pleasantly at the cute waitress as she placed their steaming meal on the table.

Terri got to POW Electronics a few minutes past four. The sign said closed but some of the employees were still there, getting ready to leave. She knocked on the glass door. She watched as Roger, the sales representative that had attended to her a couple days ago, smile and walk over to the door.

"Hi, Ms. Miller," he gushed. "A pleasant surprise...we're closed but come on in."

"Thank you, Roger," Terri said, as she stepped inside. She walked over to where they had seating for the customers and indicated for Roger to sit next to her. He waved goodbye to three employees who were leaving and sat down next to Terri.

"Having a problem with the equipment?" Roger asked as he sat down.

"As a matter of fact I do," Terri replied. "I need to speak with technician who did the installation. Was it you?"

"No, usually it would be," Roger told her, "but when I was getting ready to go up there, the general manager told me that it was already taken care of."

Terri's pulse quickened.

"Was the general manager the one who did the installation?"

"Well…I don't know for sure…he just said that it was already taken care of," Roger said. "What's the problem you're having? I can deal with it right now if you like Ms. Miller."

Terri smiled. *Such a nice young fellow*, she thought. *Fortunately for him he doesn't seem to be involved in whatever the hell is going on.*

"Thank you but what I really need is to have a word with the technician that came to my home. Is the general manager here?"

"No, he left earlier in the afternoon," Roger said, rising. "Let me see if I can get him on his mobile."

Terri waited impatiently while he made the call. She just *knew* that she was at pivotal juncture in the case.

Chapter 22

"Fuck me harder Patrick!" Cassandra, the receptionist at POW Electronics commanded as Patrick did his utmost best to comply with her request. They were at their usual rendezvous, the Elixir Hotel on South Camp Road. Cassandra was on her hands and knees and Patrick was behind her, his movements a blur as he drove in and out of her with wild abandon.

"Don't bloodclaat stop!" Cassandra growled through gritted teeth when she heard his cell phone ringing.

Patrick grunted as he tried valiantly to delay his orgasm. Cassandra was insatiable and he did not have time to recuperate and give her another round. He was supposed to accompany his wife to an art exhibition at 7 p.m. He wondered, and not for the first time, how he had come to be so smitten by the voluptuous, experienced beyond her years, 19 year old. She was the same age as his first daughter. He would give her anything she wanted, and what she wanted was a red 2005 Honda Civic that she had seen at one of the car dealerships on Hagley Park road. He had promised his wife a vacation to London this year but it would have to wait. The deposit for the car was three hundred and fifty thousand dollars and he was planning to make the payment this coming Wednesday.

"Yes Patrick! Just like that! Oh god Patrick! Right there!" Cassandra squealed with pleasure, as she backed her ample ass up against Patrick, meeting him stroke for stroke. She was feeling particularly energetic, as Patrick had given her the good news of his intention to make the deposit on the car on in a few days. She couldn't wait to drive it off the lot.

Patrick moaned loudly, unable to hold back any longer. He wondered if he could come up with a good excuse to give his wife in order to miss the art exhibit.

Roger shook his head from over by the receptionist's desk.

"He's not answering his phone," he said. Roger knew where he was, but it would complicate things if he told Terri. Roger was also seeing Cassandra, though they were trying to keep it under wraps until she got everything she could out of Gordon.

"I need his number and address," Terri said to Roger, adding, "and when you do speak to him, keep the purpose of my visit here to yourself, or you could find yourself behind bars for interfering in police business."

Roger's eyes widened at that. What the hell was going on?

"No, Ms. Miller, I definitely won't say anything."

Roger gave her the general manager's name and mobile numbers but was unable to supply the address. Roger knew that he lived in the Red Hills Road area but did not know the exact address. Terri thanked Roger for his help and headed back to Police Headquarters. Terri thought the man's name sounded familiar but she couldn't put her finger on it. She would try calling him again in a little while. It was critical that she speak with him as soon as possible. Terri then called Detective Foster and told him to meet her at her office in half an hour. She needed to bring him up to date on everything that had happened on her end since they last spoke. She thought of the *Wolf Man* as she stopped at the stop light at Ruthven Road. She wondered what his sick, depraved ass was up to right at that moment. She couldn't wait until the day she met him face to face. He would be a dead man.

Chapter 23

nna did not like the vibe she was getting from her dinner companion. At first, she had been enjoying his company and had decided that if he suggested it, she would have been game for an evening romp in the sack, but that feeling had changed over the last few minutes. She couldn't quite put her finger on it but something was suddenly off. He seemed very preoccupied and distant though he was pretending to listen to her, and there was a look in his eyes that though she could not read, made her very uncomfortable.

Watson noticed the change in Anna. She had become less gregarious and kept looking at her watch. He knew that sometimes, when the itch reached fever pitch, and he was excited and frustrated about not being able to act immediately, it showed in his face and body language. He wondered if that was the case now. He knew now that he would have to use brute force with Anna, she would no longer come willingly. It didn't matter. She was coming regardless, no matter how risky the circumstances.

"Patrick Gordon?" Foster rubbed his thin goatee. "I know that name…"

"Yes, it sounds very familiar," Terri agreed.

They were in her office at Police Headquarters discussing the case. Foster was very disturbed about the cameras Terri had found in her apartment. Talking to this Patrick Gordon was of paramount importance.

"Excuse me for a minute…I'm going to check on something," Foster told Terri and left her office.

Terri booted up her laptop and quickly typed up a status report to give to the Commissioner. She didn't have to but she liked to keep him in the loop. The information it contained was too sensitive to give her secretary to type so she did it herself.

When Foster returned, Terri had finished the report and was looking out the window, wondering if the bastard was going to strike tonight. Foster was smiling and holding a file in his hand.

"Look what I found," he said in a pleased voice.

Terri took the file from him. She grinned as she looked in it.

"You're the best," she said to Foster.

It was the personnel file for Patrick Eugene Gordon, former constable in the Jamaica Police Force. He had retired four years ago at the age of thirty-six. Terri now remembered why his name was familiar. He was one of four policemen that had been tried for the murder of an alleged gunman. They had all been acquitted and Gordon had quit the force a year later. He was married with three children, two girls and a boy. Now he was the general manager for POW Electronics. He also had very important information to provide to his former place of employment. Roger had told her he lived in the Red Hills road area which was not the address on the file. Apparently he had moved in the years since his retirement.

"I'm going to try him again," Terri said to Foster and reached for her cell phone. If she didn't get in touch with him via phone, she would have to wait until Monday and go down to his workplace. She could not wait that long to talk to him. If her instincts were right, it could be a matter of life and death.

Watson finished his meal and watched as Anna placed her knife and fork across her plate, indicating that she was through. She had barely touched her food.

"Didn't like the dish?" Watson asked, looking at her intensely.

"No," Anna lied. "Matter of fact, I'm not feeling too well, I think I'm going to have to end this date earlier than expected."

Watson's eyes narrowed briefly before he smiled sympathetically.

"Ok," he nodded agreeably. "Let's go."

He left sufficient cash on the table to cover the meal and they walked out slowly to the parking lot. Anna felt very nervous. She couldn't explain it but it was like he was transforming before her very eyes. His whole aura was suddenly menacing, even when he smiled. There was no warmth in it. It was faker than her friend Tasha's boobs.

It was now 5:15 p.m. and the late evening sun was still shining brightly, however, Anna did not see anyone in the parking lot. Cursing her luck, and feeling very afraid, she casually reached for her cell phone the same time she extracted her car keys from her pocketbook. Why was she so suddenly scared of this man? She could not articulate her fear if her life depended on it. But *something* was wrong. He stood close to her when they got to their vehicles. He deactivated the alarm on his SUV but continued to focus his attention on her. Anna flashed a weak smile and casually scrolled to her address book and selected Terri's number.

"I'm sorry we had to end the date prematurely but I'll take your number as soon as I finish this call," Anna said to him as she prayed that Terri answered her phone.

Watson smiled as his eyes quickly darted around the parking lot. An elderly couple had just exited a beige Mercedes sedan. Fuck 'em. It was now or never.

Chapter 24

"Shit! He's not picking up and I don't want to leave a message," Terri said to Foster. "I don't want to alarm him."

"Yeah, guess all we can do is keep trying," Foster replied, as he rose to leave. "I'm also going to ask around…maybe he had some good friends on the force that he still keeps in touch with."

Terri nodded and went into her private office bathroom to pee. She could hear her cell phone ringing where she left it on the desk.

Watson suddenly crushed Anna in a bear hug with his left hand, cradling her against his chest as he choked her with his right. Anna held on tightly to the phone as she struggled to breathe.

"Listen to me carefully bitch," Watson whispered coldly in her ear. "We're going inside the back of my truck. Do not struggle or I will snap your fucking neck like a twig. You dig?"

With that he released her neck and Anna gasped for air. Still hugging her to his chest, he opened the right back door and flung her into the vehicle, stepping in behind her and closing the door.

He couldn't bother to take her home. He would violate her right here and beat the living shit out of her for ruining the evening.

"Isn't that Anna's car?" Barrington Miller, Terri's father said to his wife. They had come to the restaurant, which was one of their favourite places to eat, after leaving Terri's apartment. Mr. Miller had seen a man and a woman go into the Range Rover parked next to the Lexus but he wasn't sure if the woman was Anna. The woman had seemed to be ill or something as she had been slumped against the man's chest.

"Hmmm…I'm not sure," she replied. "But anyhow, I'm sure Anna wouldn't appreciate us butting into her business and I'm hungry…so let's go eat."

Barrington took a parting glance at the two unmoving vehicles and held his wife's hand as they went inside the restaurant.

Watson locked the vehicle and started the engine with the remote on his key ring. Anna was curled up against the door shivering with terror as her mind struggled to come to terms with what was happening. If only she had excused herself and gone to the bathroom and called Terri. Or just get up and ask one of the waiters to escort her to her car. Anything but this. She had not terminated the call when Terri's voicemail had chipped in. She could only pray Terri would hear something useful when she checked her voicemail. What the hell was he going to do to her? When he turned around and she saw the look on his face she knew the answer.

Terri exited the bathroom and picked up her phone. She checked to see who had called. Anna. There was a voice message.

Terri listened, frowning. There was a low male voice saying something she couldn't quite make out and there was the rustling of fabric, gasping, a door opening and shutting, and the sound of an engine being switched on, then music before the message ended. Anna was definitely in trouble. She quickly dialed Anna's number. She didn't expect her to answer but what else could she do? She had no idea where Anna was.

Anna was vaguely aware that her phone was ringing. The beast was astride her plunging mercilessly. She was in terrible pain. He had beaten her viciously before he started raping her. She had screamed so loudly after he punched her in the ribs that she had expected someone to come to her rescue. He had punched her in the mouth, silencing her. Her lips were extremely swollen and she wasn't sure if she had swallowed some blood and a tooth. She thought so. She figured her ribs were broken. The pain she felt in her side every time he moved inside her was unbearable. She could barely see out of her eyes. He had punched her face repeatedly until she thought he was going to kill her. She became vaguely aware that he was biting her in the neck. She supposed it hurt but her entire body was already in so much pain it didn't make a difference. Maybe he was climaxing. She wasn't sure.

Watson growled in her ear after he was through and had fixed his clothes. Blood dripped from his mouth as he spoke.

"Tell your friend that she's next."

With that he calmly threw her out of the vehicle and she fell to the hard concrete with a thud. She did not move. Watson then casually drove out of the parking lot. He hadn't even looked around to see if anyone was watching. Such was the feeling of invincibility. It was his world. Everyone else was just in it. He headed home to relax and clean up.

Terri could not concentrate on anything from the moment she had listened to the disturbing sounds on her voicemail. Her best friend whom she loved like a sister was in trouble and she did not know how to proceed. She felt so helpless. She dialed Patrick Gordon's number again. Still no answer. Sighing, Terri gathered her things and left the office. She decided to go home for a bit. Playing with Marc-Anthony would help to take off some of the edge.

Gordon sighed contentedly. He was still at the hotel with Cassandra. They were now having a drink from the bottle of white wine he had bought. He looked at all the missed calls. The office and a number he did not recognize that had called his phone four times. The person hadn't left a message. Oh well, if it was important they would call back. It was now 5:45. He either needed to call his wife with an excuse or get up and get going. He pondered for another 5 minutes until Cassandra made up his mind for him. She got up and padded sexily to the bathroom. He watched her naked frame until she disappeared into the bathroom, closing the door behind her. Gordon knew he was getting too caught up with a girl young enough to be his daughter but he couldn't help it. It was as if the sun rose and settled between her legs. Being inside her was heaven on earth. He took up his phone and dialed his wife's number. He would tell her an important client had a malfunction in their security system and he had to go up there to deal with it. He knew she hated to go anywhere late so she would not wait on him. Cassandra exited the bathroom and Gordon raised a finger to his lips indicating for her to be quiet as his wife came on the line.

"Oh my god..." a woman whispered in horror at the sight of Anna's bloody, unconscious, half-naked body laying on the ground.

"Get in the car kids!" she shouted at her two children as she opened the back door of her Dodge Caravan and locked them in. She ran out to the gate to get the security guard as she frantically dialed 119.

Terri was home watching cartoons with Marc-Anthony when she got the call. She looked on the caller ID. Detective Foster.

"Hello."

"It's me…I'm afraid I have some bad news…your friend, Anna Winslow, is at the hospital," Foster told her softly. "She's in critical condition."

Terri closed her eyes and said a quick prayer. Thank god she was alive.

"Which hospital?" Terri asked in a strained voice, already getting up to give the baby to Mavis.

"Caribbean University…I'll meet you up there," Foster told her and hung up.

Terri hurried out to her SUV and headed to the hospital. The past two weeks had been like something out of a movie – a horror movie.

Foster was already at the hospital when she got there. Terri spoke to the head nurse quickly and was allowed to go the room where they were preparing Anna for surgery. Terri tried to hold back the tears but couldn't when she saw Anna. She broke down and had to be escorted from the room. Dr. Williams, the doctor in charge, led her to his office to speak with her.

Just as Terri dried her eyes and composed herself, she saw something that made her heart skip several beats. On the doctor's desk was a photo of himself, a woman and a baby. It was as if she was looking at a picture of her son, Marc-Anthony.

Chapter 25

Watson wasn't entirely pleased with the day's work but he had achieved some measure of satisfaction from his attack on Anna.

Bet your smug, shallow ass won't be so uppity now, he thought as he stripped off his dirty, bloody clothes and went into the bathroom to take a shower. He planned to stay in and relax tonight. Maybe read a book. He couldn't wait to see the papers in the morning. The name *Wolf Man* would be on everybody's lips.

"Dr. Williams," Terri said softly. "Is that your family?"

He looked at the photo and beamed proudly.

"Yes," he replied. "That's my lovely wife and our son."

Terri desperately wanted to ask if he was the biological father though she could never be that rude. Anyways it was obvious that he was not. The baby looked just like Anthony. Just like Mavis had said. Terri took a deep breath and tried to focus on the matter at hand. She would have to think about the disheartening discovery later. Right now her best friend was in a serious condition and she needed to know what had happened.

"What happened to Anna?" Terri asked the doctor.

Dr. Williams sighed and took up his notes.

"She has survived a brutal attack but her condition is quite serious. She was raped and severely beaten. Her jaw is broken, her ribs are broken in two places on the right side, her left eye requires surgery quickly or she will lose it, and there is a really nasty wound to her neck. She also received a hard blow to the head, which, along with the trauma associated with the attack, has caused her to be comatose."

Oh my God, Terri thought. *Poor Anna.*

"We have all the relevant experts on hand...we'll have to start operating immediately," the doctor advised.

Terri nodded solemnly. This was the final straw. She had to catch this inhumane maniac and soon. She was going to hold a press conference tomorrow at 12 noon. When the papers came out in the morning, there would be pandemonium. She would have to reassure the public that the police was on top of the case and she would also send him a direct message. One he couldn't ignore. She was also going to somehow find Patrick Gordon within 24 hours.

Gordon finally left the hotel at 8:30. He was completely sated. He figured his wife wouldn't be back until about 10. Plenty of time for him to go home and clean up and relax until she got home. He hoped she wouldn't want any tonight. He had no more to give. He dropped Cassandra at her home where she lived with her mom and younger sister, and then headed home. He arrived at the three bedroom dwelling in ten minutes. He parked in the garage; his wife would park behind him in the driveway when she got home. Gordon hummed as he opened and closed the grill on the verandah. He went into the dark house and switched on the living room light as he closed the door. He gasped in shock when he turned around. His wife was sitting on the couch.

Chapter 26

orraine!" Gordon exclaimed. "Yuh frighten mi."

She did not respond. She simply sat there with her stout legs crossed and looked at him.

"I thought you were at the exhibition…why yuh here sitting in the dark?" he asked nervously. *Jesus Christ…I wonder if I can pass her and go into the bathroom and take a quick shower,* he thought inwardly.

"So where are the kids?" he asked as he tried to casually walk by the sofa where she was sitting. "And where is your car?"

Lorraine watched her partner for the last twenty years and husband for the last ten, squirm with guilt. She had known about the affair, his first to her knowledge, for two months now and she realized that it was getting out of hand, threatening their family structure. Pretending it didn't exist was no longer an option. It was time for confrontation.

"You were out fucking your little office tramp again I assume?" Lorraine stated matter-of-factly.

Gordon's jaw dropped in shock. *How the hell did she know?*

"Lorraine! What happen to you woman?" he protested. "Yuh gone mad?"

She got up suddenly and grabbed him.

She slapped him in the face.

"I can smell the stink of your sex," she said contemptuously. "You must think I'm stupid Patrick."

Gordon decided that offense was the best defense. He grabbed his wife by her blouse.

"Hey woman, ah wey yuh a deal wid. Eeeh?" he asked rhetorically. "Come ah put yuh hand inna mi face an' ah accuse mi of foolishness."

"Let go of me…you fucking idiot," she said, shoving him away. "The little young girl is just using your stupid ass. You should be ashamed of yourself. She's young enough to be your fucking daughter. Have you no self-respect?"

Her words stung Gordon. Enraged, he slapped her on the mouth. It was the first time he had ever laid hands on her. Shocked but resolute, Lorraine did not back down. She jumped on him and they toppled over, smashing onto the coffee table. Lorraine scratched, clawed and punched him until he roared and flung her off him. She hit her head on the floor hard.

"Mi ah go teach yuh a lesson, come ah chat fuckery ah mi ears," Gordon said, in heat now and convinced this was the only way to deal with this. If push came to shove he would leave her rass. Cassandra would be more than happy to have him all to herself.

He pulled her off the floor and slapped her a few more times. Crying, with a growing lump on her forehead, Lorraine fought back.

"You're going to jail tonight! I swear to God I'm going to report this to police!" she cried.

His chest heaving, Gordon pushed his wife to the floor. There was no turning back now. He knew she would never forgive him for this. He loved his family but Cassandra had given him a new lease on life. He felt emotions and was experiencing a level of stamina that he thought were things of the past. He felt reborn. Revitalized. Virile. Desired. A separation wouldn't be too hard on the kids. His eldest daughter was away at University, and the middle child was in her final year in high school. Little Patrick Jr. would be affected the hardest, but in time, he would be ok without having his daddy around all the time. Life was about change after all, wasn't it? He wasn't concerned about her declarations of involving the police. He still had friends in the force and the Jamaica Police Force took care of its own. Nothing would come of it. He turned from his wife, ignoring the pain and betrayal evident in her eyes, and went into the bedroom to pack some of his clothes. He would chill over his best friend's place for a few days. Maybe take a trip with Cassandra to Miami for a week and give her the good news. She wasn't yet due for vacation leave but he was the general manager, he could approve it. He was sure she would be thrilled.

Chapter 27

erri went to the scene of Anna's attack after she left the hospital. She went inside and asked for the manager. The manager, a lovely Indian woman dressed in traditional garb, led Terri around the back to her office so they could speak in private.

"Terrible what happened, isn't it?" she began as they sat on the small couch in front her desk. She was visibly shaken about the attack. "I'll have to beef up security on the premises. This is really frightening. Do you know if she's alive?"

"She's alive," Terri replied solemnly. "Do you have any information at all that might be useful?"

"Yes," the manager replied, nodding her head enthusiastically, happy to help. She had met them at the door and had already spoken to the waitress who had attended to their table. "She came in with a gentleman sometime after four p.m. They didn't stay very long...maybe forty minutes or so."

"Describe her companion."

The manager thought for a moment.

"He was tall and well-built...attractive...well-dressed," she said.

"How did he pay for their meal?" Terri asked. The description fitted the person who had delivered the grotesque package to Police Headquarters. Just as she thought, the cheeky bastard had done the delivery himself.

"He had left some cash on the table…seems they left in somewhat of a hurry…the lady's food had barely been touched," the manager related.

"You have been most helpful," Terri said, rising to leave.

"Another thing," the manager said. "That same man was here before. I remember because he had asked the waitress to speak with the owner and when I went to him he had been very complimentary about the dish he had ordered. The same dish he ordered today for both of them. He seems to be an American."

"Why do you think so? His accent?" Terri asked.

"Yes…he definitely sounds American," the woman confirmed.

"Thank you so much," Terri said, giving her a quick hug. "Fear not…we're going to get him…real soon."

"I have all the faith in the world that you will," she replied.

Terri said goodbye and went outside to speak with the security guard. This guy was really brazen, Terri thought as she walked out to the security booth. It was obvious that the egotistical psycho gave little thought to the notion of getting caught. Good. It would prove to be the death of him.

There were now two security guards at the gate. The lone guard that was on duty earlier was one of them. Terri spoke to him for a few minutes. He wasn't much help but at least she now knew the make of the man's vehicle. It was the last vehicle to exit the premises before the woman had discovered Anna's body and raised the alarm. A Range Rover Sport. Black and chrome. Too bad they didn't record the license plate numbers of the vehicles that entered the premises. Terri thanked him and left. She called home to speak to Mavis as she drove out.

"Mavis," Terri said when came on the line. "Describe the technician that did the installment at the house a couple days ago."

Mavis told her what she remembered.

"Did he have a foreign accent?" Terri asked hopefully.

"Yes Ms. Terri," Mavis replied.

Bingo. Terri's adrenaline was pumping at high speed as she terminated the call. She was at that euphoric junction where all the pieces were coming together and the next step would lead to busting the case wide open. The psychotic murderer was definitely linked to POW Electronics. It wasn't Patrick Gordon though, as the picture Terri saw on his police file did not match the description of the killer. However, Gordon could lead them to him. Terri felt giddy with excitement. She was almost there. She called Foster to update him.

Chapter 28

was just about to call you," Foster said. "The dispatcher just got a 119 call from a woman who says she was assaulted by her husband. Guess who it is?"

Terri thought for a moment.

"Gordon's wife?"

"And the winner is…" Foster joked. "Yep. The address is 10 Moffat Drive. That's off Red Hills road. Take the immediate left turn after you pass Red Hills Mall."

"Great! Meet you there," Terri said as she turned in that direction. Things were really coming together. *I'm really coming for you now you psychotic animal*, Terri mused as she waited at the traffic light on Trafalgar Road. *Can you hear my footsteps?*

"What a gwaan, man," Detective Corporal Ronald Stern said as he greeted his long time good friend Patrick Gordon. Gordon had called him saying he needed a place to crash for a few days until he sorted out a few things. Stern alone lived in a four bedroom house that had been willed to him by his grandfather so he didn't mind. He had acres of space.

"Bwoy…Lorraine find out 'bout Cassandra and we just have a big fight," Gordon replied as he stepped in the house with his bag.

"Rassclaat!" Stern exclaimed. "How yuh manage mek she find out?"

"Mi nuh know how she find out," Gordon told him. "She just attack mi wid it and worse mi did ah come from the hotel smelling like pussy. De woman siddung inna de dark house ah wait pon mi. Yuh can believe dat?"

Stern laughed boisterously. He loved this kind of thing.

"Anyway, mi was just about to go to Buckingham Royale with Eastwood and Gregory fi go get couple lap dance when yuh call. So come we leave out now. Yuh can give me the details on the way."

Gordon placed his bag in one of the bedrooms and they hopped in his car and drove to Buckingham Royale, one of Kingston's most popular strip clubs, to meet the other guys.

Terri arrived at the address and parked outside the gate. Foster pulled up just as she exited the vehicle and activated the alarm. They entered the premises cautiously, wary of any dogs. They got to the verandah and Foster knocked on the grill. A woman opened the front door and looked out. She was crying and on the phone.

"JPF Ma'am," Terri said. "We're responding to the assault call…"

The woman said something on the phone and hung up. She wiped her face and came out to the grill.

She was startled to see that it was Terri Miller. What was such a big wig in the force doing answering a domestic assault call?

She opened the grill and let them in.

Terri introduced herself and Foster, and they followed her inside. They looked around the living room and took pictures of the smashed furniture, coffee table, broken lamp and scattered magazines. They took pictures of her swollen right cheek and the large lump on her forehead and then they took her statement.

"Where is your husband now Mrs. Gordon?" Terri asked when they were through.

"I have no idea," she replied. "He packed some of his clothing and left immediately after the fight."

Terri was happy that fate allowed them to be the ones that responded to the call. If Gordon still had friends in the force and they had been the ones to come here, nothing would have been done. She would ensure that Gordon got what was coming to him.

"Do you know his close friends?" Terri queried.

"She thought for a moment.

"Not really...his friends don't usually come here," she replied.

"Ok," Terri said, rising to leave. "Don't worry, we are going to issue a warrant for his arrest once the paperwork is done up tomorrow."

Terri and Foster told her goodbye and made their way out to their vehicles.

Lorraine closed the grill and went back inside the house. She wondered if she was doing the right thing. After all, they had been together for so long and he was the father of her children. This was the worst thing he had done in all their years together. Maybe if he ended the affair with the young girl she could forgive him and they could get past this. Maybe she was too hasty in calling the police. Gordon was a good man. The young witch probably just had him under her spell, causing him to want to desert his family. She was happy that she had taken Patrick Jr. and his sister to their aunt's for the night. She needed to think.

Watson put down the book he was reading, a novel by an obscure Nigerian author, and went into the den to pour himself a drink. He then went into the control room, he wanted to see if anything was going on at Terri's home. He frowned as he clicked to all the areas where he had installed the hidden cameras. Nothing but darkness.

What the fuck, he growled inwardly. *Had she somehow found them?* He flung his drink into the wall in anger. This was not a good development. If she had found them she would know that the technician from POW Electronics must have been the one to put them there. Had she already paid POW a visit? Most likely not. The police would have showed up here already. There was time to salvage the mess. Patrick Gordon was the only person at the office who knew him and knew that he had been the one to do the installation. He would have to kill Gordon. Watson quickly got dressed and dialed Gordon's home number. The line was busy. He called Gordon's mobile. No answer. He decided to go by Gordon's house. He was furious as he headed out to Red Hills road. How the fuck did that bitch find the cameras?

Chapter 29

erri and Foster went to Police Headquarters after they left Gordon's house. They were in Terri's office nursing two large mugs of steamy Blue Mountain coffee and ginger muffins. They were discussing the case from top to bottom, trying not to leave any stones unturned. Gordon still wasn't answering his phone.

"One of the Sergeants told me that Gordon and Stern were good friends while he was in the force but he doesn't know if they still keep in touch," Foster said.

Terri grunted. She knew Stern wouldn't tell them shit, even if he didn't know why they were asking. Terri knew he hated her guts. She had heard about Foster's run in with Stern the other day. She smiled inwardly but didn't say anything about it to Foster. She knew he would feel embarrassed.

"So much for that," Terri said wryly.

Terri placed her cup down as something dawned on her.

"Oh shit, Foster," she groaned.

"What...you ok?" he asked, alarmed.

"I just realized something...when the killer realizes that the cameras he placed in my home are no longer there..."

Foster knew exactly where she was going.

"He knows that it will easily be traced back to POW…" he filled in.

"And will know that it is only a matter of time before we find out his identity…"Terri continued.

"So the only thing to do is to eliminate the person who knows who did the installation…" Foster added.

"So we have to get to Gordon before he does…" Terri concluded.

They were both silent as they pondered the situation. Easier said than done. Gordon was proving to be more slippery than an eel, though unwittingly, Terri was certain. He had no way of knowing the police was looking for him.

"Go back up to his house and ask his wife if she has heard from him," Terri told Foster. "I doubt it but in any case take two constables with you, go in a plain car and stake out the house until you hear from me. He might return there during the course of the night."

Foster nodded and left to do her bidding.

Watson got to Gordon's house and parked his Range Rover outside on the side of the road. He had called Gordon's mobile twice on his way there but still no answer. He exited the vehicle and went into the yard. There were lights on inside the house. Somebody was home.

Foster rounded up two constables and they hopped in one of the assigned plain police cars, a 2007 tinted Toyota Corolla, and headed out to Red Hills Road.

"Hello?" Watson called out when he got to the grilled verandah. When no answer was forthcoming, he rapped on the grill several times.

The incessant knocking awakened Lorraine. She had dozed off on the couch after taking some Advil. The stress of everything had brought on a painful headache.

She checked the time. It was 10 p.m. Frowning, she got up and opened the front door.

"Yes?" she enquired in a tone showing her displeasure at this late, unexpected visit.

Watson turned on the charm.

"My sincere apologies for disturbing you," he said, flashing a bright smile. "I'm trying to locate Patrick Gordon. I'm his boss and I need to speak with him urgently."

Lorraine was surprised. The well-spoken, attractive man seemed very young to own such a successful business. Patrick was well-paid.

"Hi, nice to meet you," Lorraine replied. "I'm his wife, Lorraine."

Watson offered his hand through the grill.

Lorraine, embarrassed, opened the grill and allowed him to come in.

"Pardon me for forgetting my manners," she apologized as she shook his hand.

Watson merely smiled.

"Patrick isn't here," she told him. "And I don't where he is at the moment."

Watson was getting angry. This was not what he wanted to hear. The stupid woman had no idea where her husband was on a Saturday night?

"May I use your phone please? The battery on my cell phone has died," he said to her.

"Sure," Lorraine said, leading him inside. Watson pulled the door shut behind him and quickly grabbed her from behind, clamping his hand tightly over her mouth as he removed the blade from his pocket.

Foster instructed the two constables to stay in the car and be alert. He then made his way towards the house. He called out several times but there was no answer. Several lights were on and he thought it unlikely with the high cost of electricity these days due to rising oil prices that Mrs. Gordon would have left the house like that. He rapped on the grill and realized that it was not padlocked. He opened it and made his way to the front door. After knocking several times and getting no response, he tried the lock. The door was open. Foster pulled his firearm and entered the living room. Mrs. Gordon's bloody corpse greeted him.

Chapter 30

Watson was edgy as he drove to New Kingston. Gordon still wasn't answering his phone and he had no idea where to find him. He doubted the cops had gotten to him yet but it wouldn't be too long before they did. He had to find him first. But where was the bastard? He decided to take the edge off by having a drink. He turned on Ruthven Road and headed to Buckingham Royale. Maybe a few drinks and a quickie with a hot stripper in the VIP room would do the trick.

"Oh my God," Terri said, when Foster informed her of his gruesome discovery. The poor innocent woman. He went there and didn't find Gordon so he killed the man's wife. That cold-blooded bastard. Terri hung up from Foster and exhaled deeply as she stood by the window. She was so close. All she had to do was find Patrick Gordon and everything else would fall in place. She checked the time. It was 10 p.m. The papers would be out soon. There was going to be pandemonium when the public saw The Gleaner's sordid front page story. Terri made a decision. She would put out an all points bulletin on Patrick Gordon. She was determined to have him in custody tonight. She picked up the phone to issue instructions to the dispatcher.

Chapter 31

ordon smiled drunkenly as the skinny but gorgeous stripper gyrated sensuously on his lap. He was rock hard. This was his second lap dance of the night. His friend Stern had treated him to the first, done by a jet-black young stripper from rural Hanover. He had enjoyed feeling her firm, juicy ass grinding on his en-clothed member but it didn't compare to the one he was getting now. The combination of the stripper's extraordinarily pretty face and exquisite movements was pushing him over the edge. He didn't want to climax in his trousers. He pulled her head down to his.

"How much fi go inna de VIP room?" he slurred.

"Fifteen hundred for access and the balance depends on what we are going in there to do…" she told him, breathing in his ear seductively.

Gordon groaned in heat as he tried to remember how much money he had in his wallet. He figured he had at least six thousand left. If he needed more he could borrow it from Stern.

"I want to fuck baby," Gordon told her of matter-of-factly.

The stripper smiled inwardly. This would be a quick and easy five thousand dollars. He wouldn't last long. She was sure she could make him climax in five minutes.

"No problem...five thousand," she whispered, flicking her tongue in his ear.

Gordon almost ejaculated.

"Ok," he replied in a strained voice.

"Mi soon come back," he said to Stern and the other guys as the stripper led him to the VIP room.

"Tek time wid 'im!" Stern shouted boisterously over the din of the music being played, before turning his attention back to the main stage where four new dancers had just started their routine.

The long-legged stripper led Gordon through the crowded club to the back where the VIP room was located. A burly, bald-headed security guard was at the entrance. His black T-shirt, with the word *Security* emblazoned in the middle, was a tight fit. He smiled at the stripper.

"Melissa yuh look good tonight as usual," he said as Melissa rubbed his massive chest playfully.

"Thanks Oliver," she purred as she gestured for Gordon to pay the access fee. Gordon managed to extract the money from his wallet and hand it to the guard, who snatched it from his hands and slapped Melissa on her tiny butt playfully as they walked pass him and entered the room.

The VIP room was softly lit with red lights and was sectioned off into four areas, the entrance to each area covered by a drape. A closed drape meant that the section was occupied. The stripper led Gordon to one of the two unoccupied sections. They went in and she pulled the drape shut. She gently pushed Gordon down on the small leather couch and held out her hand for payment.

"You have to pay before," she told him with a disarming smile.

Gordon forked over the money.

She counted it, frowning slightly when she realized it was only $4500 and not the full $5000. Gordon ignored her, and hurriedly slipped his pants and briefs to his ankles, freeing his stubby, turgid dick. It was slick with pre-cum.

Melissa sighed as she slipped off her panties. She hated being shorted. Even if it was a dollar, much less five hundred. But she wouldn't make a big deal about it. One of the man's companions, a detective named Stern, was bad news. It wouldn't pay to get on his bad side over a small amount of money. She placed a condom on Gordon's dick and straddled him as she held his dick with her right hand and positioned it at the entrance of her orifice. She continuously lubed herself throughout the night, especially when the club was busy, so he slid inside of her easily.

"Ohhhh…" Gordon groaned as she cupped his face with both hands and clenched and unclenched her pelvic muscles as she rode him slowly but forcefully.

"You like my pussy?" she whispered in his ear as she increased her tempo.

"Oh yes…yes…yes to rass…"Gordon replied through gritted teeth as he fought unsuccessfully to delay his climax. He mauled Melissa's small, pert breasts as he climaxed noisily. He had only been inside her for two minutes.

Melissa quickly got up off him and pulled up her underwear.

"I have to get back to work," she told him and left him there, feeling embarrassed and stupid at having spent so much money for two minutes of sex. Gordon ripped the condom from his flaccid dick and angrily threw it on the carpeted floor. He pulled up his pants and fixed his clothes. *Bitch!* he fumed as he left the room. The security guard snickered as he walked by, fueling his anger and embarrassment.

Watson entered the strip club and was making his way to one of the three bars in the club when he spotted Gordon. He smiled in surprise and relief. What luck finding the son of a bitch here. The gods were definitely on his side. He watched as Gordon went over to three men and sat amongst them as they laughed at a joke. Judging by the look on Watson's face, the joke was at his expense. Watson ordered a drink, Hennessey on the rocks, as a short, voluptuous stripper walked over to him. He accommodated her, slipping two one hundred dollar bills into the waist of her red g-string panties. She did a series of gyrating moves on his pelvis in appreciation as he stood by the bar and sipped his drink, watching Gordon out of the corner of his eye. Watson was relaxed now that he had Gordon in his sights. He knew that killing Gordon would not solve all of his problems but it was a good start. The connection of the cameras found in Terri Miller's home to POW Electronics would not be eliminated with Gordon's death but he would cross that bridge when he got there. After Gordon was dead, he would figure something out. After all, he was the *Wolf Man*.

Chapter 32

"Mi soon come back," Gordon said to his companions as he rose to go to the restroom. He was still peeved over the debacle with the stripper and having to endure the merciless teasing from Stern and the others. Stern nodded, not moving his beady eyes from the large pair of breasts that were dangling in his face. The nipples were pierced and they fascinated him. He had already asked the stripper if she would come home with him. She had told him that it was possible but that she couldn't leave before 2 a.m. and it would cost him $10,000 for the night. Detective Stern had told her no problem, smiling to himself. He would take her home and have his way with her and she wouldn't get a dime. What was she going to do? Report it to the police? The irony of it made him crack a hundred watt smile. She smiled back.

Watson followed as Gordon made his way to the restroom. Gordon's mind flashed on his wife as he entered the restroom. He wondered how she was doing. A tall guy with long cornrows was by the sink washing his hands and another was just finishing up at the urinal. Gordon went into the stall where the toilet was and used his feet to lift up the seat. He vomited all the liquor he had consumed when he saw the mess someone had left behind. When he finished retching on the floor, he turned to exit the stall and his eyes widened in shock when he saw his boss standing in front of him.

"My my...look at the mess you've made," Watson commented disgustedly before plunging a long thin blade directly in Gordon's heart. In the moments before his heart stopped beating, Gordon became sober, and a million thoughts fought for clarity before he departed the world unceremoniously, his face an intricate blend of shock and confusion.

Watson left the blade embedded in Gordon's chest. He merely shoved Gordon's body closer to the wall so that he could close the door to the stall. He then washed his hands and exited the bathroom. He knew the best thing to do was to leave the scene now but the itch was rearing its ugly head. It had to be scratched. He called over the stripper whom he had tipped earlier and whispered in her ear. She then led him to the VIP area.

Damian Brand, whose close friends had taken him to the strip club for his birthday, had a little too much to drink and had a sudden case of diarrhea, discovered the body when he rushed to the restroom and ripped open the door to the stall. He was unable to contain his bowel movement when the scene inside the stall greeted him. Frightened and embarrassed, he stumbled backwards and shakily sent a text to one his friends to meet him in the restroom.

Terri was at headquarters reading one of the first copies of The Gleaner to hit the streets, when she got the call about Patrick

Gordon. She was furious at the sensational headline. It blared: *'THE WOLF MAN' TOYS WITH THE POLICE*. The article went on to explain that 'Wolf Man' was the moniker of the rapist that was terrorizing the women in Kingston and it gave the chilling details of the murder of the daughter of the wealthy socialite and her prominent husband. The article also inferred that the police were inept as the killer felt confident enough to walk in to Police Headquarters and personally deliver the woman's body parts without fear of capture.

May you burn in hell Constantine, Terri thought as she grabbed her keys and quickly made her downstairs to the parking lot. Patrick Gordon was dead. It was a loss but not a devastating one in terms of finding the killer. The key was to get the information on the ownership and all the employees of POW Electronics. That would be done early Monday morning. Terri exited the elevator and walked briskly out of the lobby and headed to her vehicle. She thought of the fact that Patrick's three children were now orphans. Both parents killed by the same man within six hours of each other. She thought of her son Marc-Anthony as she drove out into the busy early Sunday morning New Kingston traffic. It was a terrible fate to befall a child. The party goers were out in full force. Terri watched as a group of people looked at the front page of The Gleaner together on the sidewalk in front of the Shell gas station as she waited for the light to turn green. She knew they were reading about the *Wolf Man*. His moniker would be on everyone's lips by Sunday's end.

Chapter 33

"Jesus Christ! Tek time nuh man!" the stripper exclaimed as Watson, holding her wide hips in a tight grip, drove himself in and out of her with forceful, measured strokes. He ignored her, enjoying the fact that he was hurting her. Even more pleasurable for him was the knowledge that she hadn't the slightest idea that this would be her last sexual experience. He felt omnipotent. He swelled inside her even more.

Kimoy, the stripper, was beginning to regret doing business with this man. He was just too intense and …there was something else but she couldn't quite put her finger on it. He had been so nice and accommodating earlier, tipping well and flirting with her. He had been cool up until the point of penetration. It was as if he had transformed into a savage beast. She couldn't wait for him to be through. As soon as she collected her money she would go to her room and chill for the rest of the night. He was well-endowed and the way he was handling her, she knew she would be extremely sore. She felt as though he was splitting her in two. The club provided accommodation at a fee for the dancers who lived out of town. There were twelve rooms at the rear of the club. The girls could also do business with their customers back there if they so desired. Kimoy groaned loudly as Watson continued to pound her mercilessly. She braced her hands against the wall and prayed that he would climax soon. He had her perched on the edge of the small, leather sofa facing the wall. It would be the last thing she saw in her nineteenth year of existence. She gasped as Watson grabbed her throat with both hands and started to squeeze the life out of her. She tried to scream but couldn't. When she took her hands off the wall to try and pry his steely fingers away, her forehead hit the wall.

Watson grunted with pleasure as his climax approached. He squeezed her throat even harder. Remarkably, Kimoy's final thought was an irrelevant one. She wondered if the West Indies had won the final test match against South Africa earlier that day. Watson growled through clenched teeth as he spilled his seed in the latex condom, his pleasure enhanced by the stripper dying as he ejaculated. That was a first for him. He wondered why he had never done that before. He withdrew from her lifeless body and removed the condom, throwing it on her back. He then got dressed.

Terri arrived at the club ten minutes after receiving the call. As instructed, the corridor leading to the bathroom was discreetly sealed off by two officers. The only persons in the club that knew about the murder were the manager of the club, the young man who had discovered the body and the friend he had told to meet him in the bathroom. The friend, whose uncle was a policeman, had called his uncle on his mobile and his uncle had advised him to stay put. Six plainclothes detectives, including Detective Foster, had arrived at the club a few minutes later to take charge of the situation. Terri nodded to the security guard at the entrance to the club, who upon recognizing Jamaica's most celebrated law enforcement officer, quickly stepped aside and allowed her entry. He didn't know what was happening but he knew it had to be something big. There were several cops milling about watching the main entrance and exit to the club plus the contingent of detectives that had stormed in moments earlier. Now the big kahuna herself, Assistant Superintendent of Police Terri Miller was here. He wondered if it was a prostitution sting. Everyone knew that management allowed the strippers to peddle sex on the premises for a fee. Terri walked briskly through the crowd, all of whom were blissfully ignorant of what had taken place. Terri noted with surprise that there were almost as much women present as men. And several of them were interacting very intimately with the strippers. Times have really changed. The first thing that greeted Terri when she passed the two cops standing guard at the entrance to the corridor leading to the restroom was the awful smell.

"So what do we have here?" Terri said to Foster, covering her nose to combat the putrid scent permeating the area.

He explained to her the circumstances under which the body was found and that Gordon had been killed no more than half an hour ago. Terri wondered if the killer was still inside the club. She suspected he was. He would get a kick out of killing Gordon and then go have a drink and look at the dancers, without fear or a care in the world.

She looked over at the young man who had discovered the body. He was standing uncomfortably in a corner wearing a forlorn expression. His friend was beside him, admirably ignoring the stench emanating from his friend's body. *He'll never forget this birthday,* Terri mused. Discovering a dead body and defecating on himself. Terri instructed two of the junior detectives to escort the young man through the back door and take him home so he could clean up and change his clothing, before going down to headquarters to give an official statement. Terri put one of the senior detectives in charge of dealing with the crime scene and then went out into the crowd with Foster to see what they could find out. The manager of the club was a nervous wreck. The last thing he needed was this kind of incident to happen at the club.

They had recently spent a tidy sum refurbishing and enlarging the club and he didn't want anything to scare the patrons away. He counted his blessings though. It could have turned out much worse. If the person who discovered the body had ran back out to the main area screaming about a dead body in the bathroom, there would have been pandemonium.

Chapter 34

erri and Foster split up, each going either side of the club intending to meet up at the VIP room. Terri stopped at the first bar and called the female bartender over. She leaned forward, wondering where she knew the woman from. Terri flashed her ID and motioned for the woman to let her come behind the bar. She opened the door and Terri bent and entered.

"Hi," Terri said to her. "I just need to ask you a couple of quick questions."

The bartender nodded.

"Do you recall serving any male patron that had an American accent?"

The bartender thought for a moment. Her angular face screwed up in consternation. She started to shake her head then she remembered the guy who had ordered the Hennessy on the rocks. She remembered him mainly because of the diamond encrusted Rolex watch on his wrist and the fact that he had given her a big tip. Yes, he definitely had an American accent.

"Yeah…this man…had on an iced out Rolex…he sounded like 'im is American," she related.

Fantastic, Terri thought.

"What did he look like?" she asked.

"Umm...he was tall...and muscular...an' 'im look nice," the bartender replied.

"How long ago did he visit the bar?" Terri asked, her eyes scanning the club.

"Ummm...'bout a hour ago," she estimated.

"Thanks," Terri told her. "You've been a big help."

Watson watched as Terri Miller left the bar and head to his direction. After leaving the VIP room, he had stopped at the closest bar and purchased another shot of Hennessy on the rocks. After getting his drink, he had glimpsed Terri Miller at the top bar speaking to the bartender. He had stayed where he was, partially hidden by a column next to the bar, and watched her. So the bitch is here. Trying to sniff him out. The hunter would become the hunted. He was going to flush her out and kidnap her. Take her to the lair and show her the true meaning of fear and terror. Watson was so caught up watching Terri Miller that he never felt someone's eyes on him.

After a lull in the action, as the patrons waited for the next crop of dancers to take the stage, Gordon's friends finally wondered how he hadn't yet returned. Stern got up and stretched.

"Mi ah go use de bathroom," he told the others. "I'll check if 'im down by the VIP room on my way back."

The others nodded and one of them signaled one of the roving waitresses to bring them another round of beer.

Oliver, the security guard who had been on duty at the VIP
area when Watson had went back there with Kimoy, came back
to his post. He had taken a half hour break.

"Everyt'ing alright?" he asked Andre, the new security guard
who had only been working there for the past three weeks.

"Yeah, man," he replied. "Everyt'ing criss."

They chatted for a few minutes before Andre walked off to
check to see if any one else needed to be relieved.

Stern recognized one of the two men standing at the entrance
of the corridor leading to the bathroom that he was going to.

"Fletcher...what yuh doing here man?" he asked good-naturedly
as he attempted to pass by the two men.

"I'm on duty," Fletcher responded, as he impeded Stern
from entering. "No one is allowed back here now. Assistant
Superintendent Miller's orders. You have to go use another
bathroom."

Stern was incredulous as he looked at the junior detective. *Is
who this wet-behind-the-ears puppy of a cop t'ink 'im talking to
like dat?* Stern asked himself.

"Ah wonder if yuh remember dat I am your superior?" Stern
asked, puffing up his chest as he got in Fletcher's face.

Fletcher was not intimidated.

"That may be so but you are not passing me tonight. Like I
said, you have to go and use another bathroom."

Stern looked beyond the men. There was an officer with his
back towards the corridor speaking to someone in the bathroom
through the partially closed door. Stern wondered what the fuck
was going on.

His anger was mounting by the second. He couldn't believe
that this pipsqueak was attempting to deny him, a senior detective,
access to what he was sure was a crime scene.

"Watch mi an' yuh bloodclaat," Stern spat as he turned to go and get Eastwood and the rest of the men. They would come back and slap the shit out of both of them. Terri Miller's orders indeed. He would see about that. He was so angry he forgot he wanted to pee.

The two officers watched him walk away in a huff. They both knew Stern was a bully and a trouble-maker. A rogue cop who served no real purpose in the Force other than himself. It was a wonder he had survived all these years with his attitude. They knew he would be back with his buddies in tow. But all it would do is get he and his friends a suspension. They were not on duty and therefore had no right to interfere with a crime scene which was already under control.

Fletcher steeled himself for the confrontation. Knowing that he was in the right, he would take pleasure in fucking up Stern. He had it coming anyway. Especially with the way he always spoke disrespectfully about Assistant Superintendent Miller. It had been awhile since he had put his karate skills to good use.

Terri knew he was still in the club. She just *felt* **it. And her** instincts were rarely wrong. She walked slowly, looking around as she went through the crowd. *You're going down Mr. Wolf Man. Tonight.*

Detective Foster watched the tall, muscular man who was watching Terri's every move intently. It had to be *him*. Foster's adrenaline flowed as he slowly made his way towards the man, never taking his eyes off him. He was a dangerous man. Foster stepped on someone's foot and the man pushed him angrily.

"Look weh yuh ah bloodclaat go!" the man growled, his bravado fueled by alcohol and the presence of five of his friends.

"Hey!" Foster exclaimed, grabbing the man by his shirt. "Relax yourself and mind you get arrested for impeding a police officer going about his duty."

"Sorry man…mi never know seh yuh ah police," the man said apologetically.

Foster sucked his teeth in annoyance and quickly turned his attention back to where the man who he was certain was the *Wolf Man* had been standing.

He was no longer there.

Chapter 35

Watson walked right by Terri Miller as he made his way outside. She never saw him. She was on her phone, struggling to have a conversation in the noisy club. He figured it was the other cop calling to let her know that he had lost sight of him. Watson chided himself for letting his guard down like that. He had almost spotted the cop too late. If it hadn't been for the commotion between the cop and the patron, he would never have noticed him. He had looked over there when he heard the arguing and had recognized one of the men as someone he had seen sitting beside Terri Miller at the table during the press conference she had held a few days ago. It was obvious that he and Terri Miller had been circling the club from either side trying to find him. So they had some idea of what he looked like. The helper at Terri Miller's house. She must have given them a description of the technician that had done the installment, who of course, Terri Miller had correctly surmised, was the *Wolf Man*. He slowed his gait when he got outside and pretended to check messages on his PDA as he casually made his way to the parking lot across the street. There were several cops outside the club, ready to accost anyone who was acting suspiciously. They ignored him and he strolled pass them across the street into the parking lot. He got into his SUV and gunned the engine.

Terri was unable to hear what Foster was saying on the phone and by the time he got to her and was able to tell her that he had been this close to nabbing the *Wolf Man*, their quarry was long gone. Terri cursed audibly. They almost had the bastard. They walked towards the VIP area and Terri spoke with the security guard at the entrance. She described the suspect and asked the guard if by any chance he had made use of the VIP room. Oliver thought for a moment. The description sounded like the man Kimoy had taken back there.

"Yeah…sounds like the guy that had gone back there with a stripper named Kimoy," he related, stroking his goatee. "A little over half an hour ago."

Right after he left the bar, Terri thought.

"Did they both come back out?" she asked.

"I'm not sure, Miss," Oliver replied. "I went on a half an hour break shortly after they went in so someone else was at this post."

Terri thanked him and went inside the VIP room with Foster to have a look around. She hoped Kimoy was still alive but deep down she doubted it. The *Wolf Man* would have no qualms about killing her right here.

Terri heard the moans but opened the thick drapes leading to one of the four sections anyway. The man saw her first, his expression of bliss replaced by surprise, then anger, then fear when he recognized the popular police officer.

He pushed the stripper away and hastily pulled up his pants.

Terri merely looked at them both without speaking. What happened in the VIP rooms of most of the strip clubs was against the law but she had bigger fish to fry right now. She went over to the next section with Foster in tow. She gasped when she opened the drapes. Though she had expected it, she was hoping that the girl was still alive. The dead woman's body was propped up obscenely by the wall, with her head cocked at an unnatural angle. Terri sighed deeply and told Foster to deal with the scene. She was going on the street for a drive.

"Just low dat man," Eastwood said, trying to calm Stern down. This wasn't the right way to deal with the situation. Why risk a suspension or worse when they could catch the disrespectful junior detective and his partner on the street unawares and extract revenge? "Dem will get what's coming to dem in due time."

Stern was really spoiling for a fight but he saw the wisdom in Eastwood's words. He nodded and sat down and checked the time. It was 1 a.m. He would be able to leave with the stripper in another hour and blow off some steam. He wondered again where Gordon had disappeared to.

Terri walked briskly through the crowd and took a deep breath when she got outside. She had felt as though she was going to suffocate just now. All the barbaric deaths and brutality over the past week was really getting to her. She nodded yes to a constable who asked her if she was ok. She then hopped in her SUV which was parked directly in front of the club and drove out. She had no idea where she was going. She just needed to clear her head. She was so out of it she never noticed the black Range Rover that was behind her.

Watson drove slowly as he trailed Terri Miller. When he had left the club, he was going to leave the area immediately but had changed his mind. He decided to stay for awhile and wait until

Terri left the club. Maybe she would leave alone and provide him with an opportunity to nab her. It had turned out to be a good decision. She was indeed alone. He occasionally fell back and allowed one or two cars to come between them. He hummed and drummed his fingers on the steering wheel. The right moment to make a move would soon present itself. Of that he was sure. He could feel it in his bones. And his loins.

Foster called Terri to check if she was ok and to let her know that both bodies were now being discreetly removed from the club, and that he was on his way to headquarters to take statements from the young man who had discovered the first body. He was also going to do a comprehensive status report which he would leave on her desk. Terri thanked him and assured him she was fine after he asked for a second time. Without even thinking about it, she realized she was almost home. A few minutes later, she opened the gate with the remote, noting that none of the two security guards even peeped out of the booth to see who was coming in. *Probably asleep*, she mused, not pleased about that. She made a mental note to speak with the company responsible for maintaining the complex. She suddenly realized that a vehicle was behind her as she drove through and was about to close the gate.

Watson was beside himself with excitement as he drove into the complex. He knew she probably was curious that she hadn't noticed the vehicle before as he had driven with the lights off when they were the only two vehicles on the stretch that led to the complex, and hadn't turn them back on until he was actually entering the complex. He casually drove past her apartment as she parked and slid into an empty slot beside a red Audi station wagon, right next door to Terri. He prayed the occupant of the apartment didn't awaken and wonder who the hell was in their driveway. He quickly slipped on a hat he had in the vehicle and got out. Terri was on the patio about to deactivate the alarm and go inside when she glanced over at the man exiting the vehicle right next door. She had never seen that Range Rover before but she had heard that her neighbour, the Ambassador, was a homosexual so it wasn't odd to see a strange man come to his house late at night. But something clicked as the man strode over to her quickly. Though she couldn't really see his face as yet, there was something very familiar about him. She looked back at the vehicle. A black Range Rover Sport. *Oh my God,* Terri thought as her knees went weak. *It's him!*

Chapter 36

Watson changed his plans as he realized the change in Terri's body language. She knew. With two giant strides he reached her as he pulled his blade and held it at her throat. He was surprised that she was able to pull her firearm so quickly. It was pressing into his washboard stomach. They didn't speak for several seconds.

Watson inhaled her scent. Even after such a long and hectic day she smelled like a fresh bed of roses. He had a raging erection.

Terri trembled but not from fear. It was from relief. Instead of her finding him, the hunted had found the hunter. No matter. The *Wolf Man's* reign of terror would end tonight. Even if she didn't survive the next few minutes, neither would he. She tightened her grip on the gun.

Watson felt the movement.

"Easy now…little one," he said in an arrogant, amused tone.

"Do you really think you can squeeze off a shot before I slit your throat and turn your lovely son into a motherless child?"

Terri looked in his eyes. They were the eyes of a mad man. Unremarkable dark brown eyes they were, yet the insanity shone through them like two bright flash lights, announcing their owner's madness to the world.

K. SEAN HARRIS

"Put the gun down," he coaxed. "Maybe then I'll let you live...after we have some fun together of course."

Watson smiled at the look that came over her face. She was looking at him like that was the most disgusting and despicable thing she had ever heard. Oh how he would enjoy torturing this bitch. He would keep her for a couple days before sending her to eternity. He would then leave the island for awhile, spend some time travelling while keeping a close eye on the news in Jamaica. It would not be safe for him to remain here now, especially after tonight.

"In your dreams asshole," Terri replied calmly, continuing to look in his eyes. "I'm going to splatter your intestines all over my patio and take you out of your sick, sadistic misery."

Watson's eyes glazed over with anger. The cunt was not exhibiting any signs of fear. She actually thought she was going to defeat him.

Terri knew he was perturbed by her lack of fear. He was used to having the upper hand. Watching his victims squirm in terror, begging for their lives. She was torn. She wanted him to die but death seemed too easy a fate. He deserved to be castrated. He deserved to suffer. To languish in isolation in prison for the rest of his life with only bad food, rodents and nightmares of the atrocities he committed to keep him company. Her mind flashed back to a year and a half ago when she was in a similar standoff. She was forced to kill the man she loved. This time she was itching to pull the trigger. To rid the world of a scourge who should have never been in it. The metallic blade felt cold and alive against her trachea. Was this the end? No. She had her beautiful baby boy to live for. She pulled the trigger and eased back a bit just as he swiped the blade across her throat.

Chapter 37

The two security guards in the booth awakened with a jolt at the sound of the two gunshots. This was not a place one expected to hear guns being fired. They rushed out of the booth with guns drawn and made their way cautiously down to the apartments, while the senior guard used his earpiece to radio in to the police.

They moved quickly when they saw the two bodies in front of the Assistant Superintendent's apartment. She was alive but blood was seeping from her throat in copious amounts.

"Call a fucking ambulance!" the senior guard shouted to his co-worker as he tried to stem the bleeding with a large rag from his pocket.

Lights in some of the apartments had come on a few moments after the gunshots were heard. Mavis had awakened instantly. So had Marc-Anthony, who was crying loudly. She went and picked him up out of his crib and walked with him to the living room window where she peeked out discreetly. She almost dropped the baby when she saw the silhouette of the two bodies lying on the entrance of the patio. With Terri's SUV parked outside, one of the bodies had to be hers.

Watson was not yet dead but he knew he was moments away. Terri Miller had been true to her words. The contents of his stomach were indeed splattered on her patio. He still couldn't believe she had actually managed to squeeze off two shots. He hadn't gotten to slice her throat the way he had wanted to, but he knew she had to be badly wounded. He could hear the security guard talking to her, telling her help was on the way. No one had even checked to see if *he* was still alive. She had defeated him. That fact hurt almost as much as the two large holes in his stomach. Watson cursed the gods with his final breath.

Terri could feel herself losing consciousness. She fought it, fearing she would never wake up. She blacked out as she prayed to God to spare her life so that she could see her son again.

Epilogue

erri looked at her chuckling son as he played with his favourite toy, a robot which transformed into a war tanker. They were at her parents' condominium in Miami. Her mother was there as well, helping the hired nurse taking care of Terri and Marc-Anthony as Terri recuperated from her injury. Terri's trachea had been badly severed but fortunately, the team of renowned experts that had performed the follow up surgery to the initial one done in Jamaica, had been able to repair the damage. She was on three months sick leave and her mom was trying to convince her to quit the force. Terri knew she couldn't. She was a law enforcement officer through and through. There was nothing else she wanted to do. She also wanted to realize her dream of becoming the first female Commissioner of Police in the Caribbean and the youngest person to hold such a post anywhere in the world. She was sure the job would be hers in 10 years. She would only be 40 years old.

That Sunday morning, three weeks ago, when Terri killed the *Wolf Man* on her patio, was a day many Jamaicans wouldn't soon forget. The sensational story that came out in The Gleaner that day had created quite a stir, and before everyone could properly digest the article, then came the news that Assistant Superintendent of Police, Terri Miller, had killed the *Wolf Man* but had been badly injured in the confrontation. The nation prayed collectively for her speedy recovery. The hospital had to appeal to the public not to send any more flowers as there was no more space to put them. People called in to the various radio shows imploring the government to make Terri Miller a national hero. The government didn't do that but she would receive the Medal of Gallantry at a special function in her honour when she had sufficiently recovered.

The case had made international headlines. Terri's beauty and the sadistic, gruesome nature of the case were irresistible news. Even CNN and the BBC got in on the act, doing profiles on Terri and digging up background information on the *Wolf Man*. Soldiers that knew him from his army days came out of the woodwork to get their fifteen minutes of fame, granting interviews and selling photos to the media. The woman he had raped in Brooklyn over two years ago was paid a tidy sum to appear on the Larry King show. It was a media circus.

Stern was at home serving a one month suspension for pulling his firearm in a threatening manner and attacking Detective Fletcher in the locker room at Police Headquarters. Stern had been extremely upset about his good friend's Gordon's murder, and even more upset about the way Fletcher had dealt with him the night at the club, so he and Eastwood had attacked Fletcher one afternoon while he was retrieving something from his locker. Fletcher, though taken by surprise, held a black belt in karate and was able to defend himself, breaking Eastwood's shooting hand and three of the fingers on Stern's right hand. An investigation was still pending. With Stern's dubious reputation and spotty record, everyone expected him to be booted from the Force. Eastwood, his running mate, would probably suffer the same fate.

Anna was still in a coma but the doctors expected her to regain consciousness eventually. The surgeries performed on her were successful and her condition was serious but stable. She just needed to wake up. Terri was very worried about her. Suppose she was in a coma for years? How much damage had been done to her psyche? Terri knew that no matter what happened; Anna would never be the same person she was before the *Wolf Man's* attack.

Terri thought about the child Anthony had fathered with another woman. Should she meet with the mother and discuss the situation? Would it be unfair of them to deny the brothers a chance to have a relationship? It would be difficult for both mothers to look beyond their personal disappointment with Anthony – based on Mavis' account of the incident the woman had been shaken up when she saw Marc-Anthony so obviously she had not known that there was another a child – and facilitate it but Terri knew it was the right thing to do. It was like deja-vu all over again, being back in this apartment recuperating from an injury and having a decision to make. She was sure she would eventually do the right thing. She smiled weakly at her precious bundle of joy. Right now she was just happy and grateful to be alive.